CONSIDER THE GREAT PYRAMID . . .

"What will a real solar tap look like? One that gives you a continuous flow of controlled power?"

The archaeologist didn't sound like a man just asking questions. The engineer was puzzled but also pleased.

"Here, I'll show you," he said, squatting on his heels beside the crate and sketching rapidly . . . "The proportions—about like the pyramids of Egypt. It'll look like those . . . On top of the pyramid—here—will be a laser system, a coherent light beam that switches on and off in microseconds, giving a surge of power each time it's on . . . The control station will be burrowed into the center of the insulator . . . reached through angled tunnels from beneath the base . . ."

The archaeologist nodded and pulled the sketch from under the clip. "I thought so," he said. I thought that's what a solar tap would look like . . . They grew up with it then and built in stone. The power's there all right . . . They knew that then too."

"I don't think I follow you."

"Pull up a chair. Offer me a cigarette and a seat . . . I've got a story to tell you . . ."

ONLY A STORY?
JUDGE FOR YOURSELF.

To Grackin—who refused to compromise the integrity of his intelligence;

To Dea—who schooled her young in the courage to look for themselves and to credit their own senses;

And to Pops—who knew that the preconceived notion is a subtle blinder in man's search for the truth.

WALT AND
LEIGH RICHMOND

WILDSIDE PRESS

SIVA!

Introduction

The research that resulted in this book was begun in 1936.

It was a time when the naïvetés of a civilization were giving way to harsh reality; when preconceived notions that had existed as axioms of thinking for hundreds of years were being questioned; when the verities on which the peoples of the world had based their lives from generation unto generation were being shown to be fallacies, and when we were paying heavily for those fallacious axioms. .

It was after the first great planetary war, and while the second was in the making. Before the atom bomb, but after the Great Depression, through which we had just struggled.

It was a time when Academic Authority, Governmental Authority, and Tradition were first being questioned.

It is difficult to remember now just how innocent we were in those days, or how harsh were the realities that were forcing a new look.

Hitler was forcing a new look at genetics and

racism, rampant in this country until the violence of his extremes forced a public reevaluation of the principles involved. In those days of "Gentlemen's Agreements," anthropologist Margaret Mead's, pleading for racial sanity, was a voice in the wilderness.

Stalin was forcing a new look at the necessities and the hazards of industrialization as he began the murderous project of forcibly industrializing a peasant-agrarian nation so that it might stand up to the newly technological world in which it existed.

Mao Tse-tung and his revolutionaries were uniting a nation historically torn and separated against the tradition-ridden armies of Chiang Kai-shek and the arms and munitions supplied by the entirety of the "free" governments of the world.

Mahatma Gandhi was proving the massive power of masses of people, even when restrained by the principle of passive nonviolence.

Einstein was forcing a new look at the hidebound traditions of physics; Oppenheimer was translating the Einsteinian theories into practical physical equations which would put the formulations at the service of engineers.

And the bitter facts of the recent depression were forcing a re-evaluation of the economic systems into which the world had patterned itself, and which had failed miserably in the face of a burgeoning technology.

So it was a period of time during which preconceived notions—those great enemies of thinking—were being forced to the forefront and were being refuted; and during which the syllogistic patterns of thinking built upon those axiomatic preconceived notions were falling left and right, with little to replace them in the way of new axioms on which to build more valid structures of thought.

I am an anthropologist, and it seemed to me at that time, more than four decades ago, that the preconceived notions on which we had based our theories of the history of the race of man on this planet were just as fallible as the other preconceived notions that were failing the light of harsh reality.

It seemed to me, too, that an understanding of our roots was an extremely important part of the maturing process of the civilization that was so obviously going on.

The discrepancies between the history of man as taught and the evidence that could be seen written across the planet in archaeological remains was obvious. The anomalies of history—those major, provable pieces of the puzzle of man's habitation of the planet—that didn't fit the patterns outlined in the history books, were myriad.

So it was that in 1936 I began outlining a history of the race. I was trying to find the pattern of that history by examining all the pieces—those that fit and those that didn't.

When you find the right pattern, I told myself, the pieces of history will fall into place. The anomalies that you see will find their position in

that pattern. It will become a consistent whole.
When anomalies exist, the pattern is necessarily
incorrect.

The anomalies were many, but the greatest and
most obvious of these were the pyramids—
structures that we would be unable to build even
today in their original rock-massive form; structures that had originally had, necessarily, an economic reason for existence; that had served a very
basic purpose in the economy of the builders.

The pyramids had appeared relatively overnight, in the midst of what had been prior to that
time an essentially mud-hut civilization. The
longest period of time that could justifiably be
assigned to their construction was two hundred
years, and that only by historical straining.

Yet even among the pyramids there were con-
trasts. There was the great pyramid at Gizeh, the
Cheops pyramid, a geometrical perfection. And
there were its lesser, satellite pyramids. And then
there was a descending scale of lesser pyramids.

Even these were not confined to one continent.
They could be found at Angkor Wat in the Bur-
mese jungle; and in Mexico on the Yucatán peninsula.

One thing they had in common: they were all at,
or near, the 30° parallels of the planet. One thing
they had not in common: none of the structures
had the geometrical perfection nor the exactness
of construction of Cheops.

The satellite pyramids, and the lesser pyramids,
obviously served different functions than that of
Cheops.

Those anomalies alone should have been sufficient to arouse curiosity about history as told. But there was much more.

There were the Piri Reis maps, which could be physically traced back to the seventeenth century, and which had left much lighter historical traces back in time to perhaps even 3,000 B.C. . . .—maps that showed the geological structure of the planet at a time when the poles of the planet were not covered in snow and ice, and that had necessarily been surveyed if not from orbital distances, at least from aerospace. The configurations they show have only recently been confirmed.

There were the great signs and symbols on the mountain sides in Peru, the structures in the jungles of South America.

There were the outlines of the continents of this planet, obviously once one continent, and the explanations that told of a slow slippage that would not have created the mountain ranges that we see as the results of that change.

There were the myriad proofs that the planet has changed its axial tilt during near-historic times; and there were the proofs that the calendars by which we operate have not always been the same; the day nor the year the length to which we have grown accustomed.

There were the piles of mammoths frozen in mounds in the arctic areas—so quickly frozen that the grass the animals had been eating was, in many cases, still green in their stomachs, which necessitated so rapid a freezing that only liquid nitrogen or something similarly cryogenic could have accomplished it. And there were the piles of bones in caves 1,000 feet high, that included fish and mammals and man, crushed together and covered with sand.

Several years after the publication of *Siva!* under the title *The Lost Millennium*, Erich Van Däniken did an excellent job of outlining a great many of the anomalies of history at which I was looking back in 1936, and on which *Siva!* is based. I highly recommend his *Chariots of the Gods* to the student of history.

But even these were not the total of the pieces of the puzzle at which I was looking then. There was at least one set of facts which seemed to contradict itself.

Both electrical appliances and plastics were used in Crete and in ancient Egypt. King David can be shown to have had Bessemer hearth furnaces, and to have armed his soldiers with weapons of Bessemer steel.

Yet the structures—the homes and the "temples" of that entire era—were of stone, with no steel understructure.

Beryllium copper—an alloy that can be manufactured only with electricity—was used by the ancients of Egypt.

Yet still the buildings were of stone.

An anomaly of the first order.

At that time, circa 1937 by then, I could not find the pattern. The parts of the puzzle were there on the table, but the puzzle would not fit together.

Then came War II—the second great planetary war; and the frantic technological advances entailed in such a war, culminating in atomic fission.

And then came secrecy. The Secrecy Acts and

all that they entailed. The witch-hunts in the name of secrecy.

Again, it is hard to remember the outcry of those who could see the predictable results of secrecy and all its connotations. It is difficult to remember, because those outcries, by the top scientists of the country, the top economists, the top theorists, were smothered by the very legislation that they fought. The fact that they fought was one of the major secrets of the secrecy syndrome.

Yet that secrecy reaction too was probably inevitable. Too many harsh realities had forced too many changes in preconceived notions, in the axioms by which people had governed their lives.

It was a nearly planetwide reaction of "Stop the world, I want to get off."

So—the world stopped. Cold. In a cold war.

Meantime, I had met and married Walt, and we set about to live happily ever after; we did until his death in April 1977.

Walt was a research physicist, an electronics engineer, a chemist, a biochemist—a generalist.

In 1962 he was doing research in atmospheric electricity, and he developed the theory of what we called the solar tap: a source of electrical power so great that one installation, about the size and expense of a normal hydroelectric installation, could produce more electrical power than is available in the world today. The physics is exact. The power is there for the tapping.

A source of power is always a two-edged sword. It can be used for construction or for war. In this case, its deleterious aspects were even greater. Power from a solar tap would necessarily be distributed as broadcast power, which Nicola Tesla had proven could be done before 1911.

But in a steel-structured civilization, broadcast power, unless carefully handled, would resonate with the structural steel of the buildings in which this civilization and its industry are housed.

Yet—with broadcast power you could "tune in" the motor of your automobile to the power source, the way you tune in a radio. You could tune in your heating system, your electric lights, your power tools, industrial equipment used in manufacturing.

We took the research papers on the solar tap to then-President John Kennedy's science advisor in 1963. We had planned to take them to the United Nations Science Advisory Committee.

Our papers were placed under the secrecy label, and we were offered a government contract for research, which we refused. It would have placed us under the Secrecy Syndrome, in which we had refused for some years to have any part. We were told to sit down and shut up, in no uncertain terms.

But meantime I had asked Walt to map out the insulator that would be necessary at ground base for a solar tap.

He drew up the needed structure, and the results were an exact replica of the Cheops pyramid at Gizeh, complete to the internal design where the technicians would be housed; complete to the granite sheathing; to the platform topside where the laser itself would be situated; and to the well beneath the pyramid which would act as the electrical ground.

But the satellite pyramids?

With that much power, you have a landing and takeoff system that can throw spaceships into orbit without the need for any rocket assist. By electromagnetic induction/propulsion you can loft thousands of tons into orbit. To do so you need a Jacob's Ladder of laser beams.

The central pyramid—the Cheops pyramid—was the power structure. The satellite pyramids angled laser beams up into what became in effect a spiral configuration of power reaching up to orbital distances.

The pyramids in Burma and in Mexico were merely power taps, broadcasting power to a civilization. They did not need the meticulous construction of Cheops.

Given these facts, the other anomalies of history fell into place in a pattern to show what had happened and what had existed. The pattern was self-consistent throughout. There were no anomalies that we could find.

So we wrote the book, Siva! We wrote it as science fiction.

Whether the story told in Siva! approaches the actual story of the beginnings of our civilization is something for the readers to decide for themselves.

The facts on which the story is based are verifiable facts. The solar tap is a real potential to our own technology; the physics on which it is based is quite exact.

That electrical power can be distributed by broadcast has been proven, though those proofs, along with most of Tesla's work, are under the secrecy label.

The anomalies of history, mentioned so briefly here, are facts that can be verified.

And the pyramids stand today, gigantic refutations of the infantile rationalizations by which we have tried to explain our origins and the roots of our history.

Whether our own findings in the history indicated by the facts are right or wrong, *Siva!* still tells only the first of the story that we see. It does not even reach through time to the building of the pyramids; to the civilization at Crete; to the destruction of Sodom and Gommorah; or to the mining of Mars; or to the genetic research that was done, that so nearly became catastrophic.

It does not reach to the times when small groups from more highly technologically developed civilizations superimposed their power structures over the "children" growing up to their heritage of the knowledges of the Lord on this planet. They were served by those "children" and they lived in the myriad of "temples" whose remains can be found from Pagan, buried in the jungles of Burma, to Mexico, to the Andes, to ancient England and Europe.

There is nearly six thousand years of history between the time of *Siva!* and today; exciting history, adventurous history.

We had intended to write the rest of that history as a science fiction series, based on the evidence that is to be found across the face of the planet. Whether it be fact or fiction, it is an exciting story.

Yet, if we are even nearly correct in our findings, ours is a race growing into manhood and headed for the stars. It would be well to discover our roots, our heritage, our proud beginnings, and to base our actions upon fact.

Leigh Tucker Richmond

Aboard the C-Lab
Rathmann's Marina
705 South Harbor City Boulevard
Melbourne, Florida 32901

Avalanche

1

The engineer had ducked under the canopy for a coffee break and a five-minute taste of what the breeze could feel like when you were out from under the sun, so he didn't see the army-style jeep drive up. The first he knew of the archaeologist was the man's coming under the canopy to join him.

The engineer recognized the name immediately, paid it the respect that was its due, then asked the mission.

"You're putting up a solar tap." The archaeologist made it a statement, not a question, which surprised the engineer. Most people asked what the hell he thought he and his crew were up to.

"That's right. I'm planning to tap into the electrical current that exists as a potential between the Earth-ground and the ionosphere. I expect to get lots of power. It's experimental, though."

"It's a primitive tap," said the archaeologist. "It

will explode. It will probably blow up several kilometers around your base here."

The engineer looked at him, startled; "That's why we're here in the desert," he said. "We've checked. We won't be blowing up any people, and we've paid for the rights otherwise."

"What are you trying to prove?"

"That the power's there. That there's a tremendous electrical potential between Earth-ground and the ionosphere. That the Earth and the ionosphere form a sort of sphere-in-sphere capacitor fed by the solar wind, with the dense part of the atmosphere acting as a leaky dielectric between them. I'm planning to short out the 'capacitor' and prove the power's there. Lots of it. Thousands of times more power than all the generating stations in the world produce today. Once I prove the power's there, there'll be plenty of money to put up a sophisticated tap system to make the power available in a controlled manner."

"I gather that for this 'short circuit' you're just using regular surplus field wire, floated up to the twenty-five kilometer level on weather balloons?"

"That's right. The wire will explode down its entire length when the power avalanches, but it will leave a hot, ionized pathway for the electricity to ride in on. That pathway—the whole 'short circuit'—will blow out in about a quarter of a second."

"What will a real solar tap look like? One that gives you a continuous flow of controlled power?"

The archaeologist didn't sound like a man just asking questions. The engineer was puzzled, but also pleased. He pulled a pencil from his pocket.

hooked a packing crate over with his toe, and reached down a clipboard of paper from its hook on one of the canopy poles.

"Here, I'll show you," he said, squatting on his heels beside the crate and sketching rapidly. The archaeologist squatted beside him so naturally that the engineer's respect went up a notch.

"This is the insulator," he said, sketching a slightly truncated pyramidal form. "The proportions — about like the pyramids of Egypt. It'll look like those. The main one will look — well, like the Cheop's pyramid. The pyramid's the insulator — to insulate the electric current from the ground. On top of the pyramid — here — will be a laser system, a coherent light beam that switches on and off in microseconds, giving a surge of power each time it's on. The power collector and transformer and the control apparatus will be at the top of the pyramid.

"The control station will be burrowed into the center of the insulator," he said, sketching now in dotted lines over the pyramid. "It will be reached through angled tunnels from beneath the base; and there'll be resonance chambers built along the entrance tunnels — something like the silencer for a gun. That's to protect the personnel from the constant pulse of the tap, and from the effects of shock wave from any arc-over or electrical avalanche. This sketch is rough, but it gives you the idea."

The archaeologist nodded and pulled the sketch from under the clip, then rose. "I thought so," he said. "I thought that's what a solar tap would look like. The frequency control would have to be exact in this steel-based civilization. They grew up with it then and built in stone."

The engineer looked at him quizzically. "You're the first person that could even recognize that the power's there to be tapped. If I could get other people to listen and understand the theory behind what I'm doing, I wouldn't have to put up this fool twenty-five-kilometer wire on balloons."

"The power's there, all right." There was no question in the voice or manner. "The power's there. Enough to blow up Earth if it's misused."

"Nope." The engineer rose slowly, then put his foot on the packing case and leaned on his knee. "I estimate about three times ten to the twentieth watts of continuous energy, with the sun acting as the power supply and constantly resupplying it. The power will avalanche, of course, when I put up the 'short circuit' across the dielectric. But the avalanche will create a magnetic field that will react with the magnetic field of Earth, and will blow itself out with magnetic winds as soon as it reaches resonance. About that quarter of a second. It'll be an explosion about the size of Hiroshima, I estimate; but not enough to blow up anything more substantial around here than a few kilometers of desert. It's self-extinguishing."

"What would that amount of power do if it avalanched in a continuous flow?"

"Burn hell out of the spot where it touched Earth. Empty the capacitor that's the ionosphere and feed directly from the solar wind. Earth's an electric motor, you know, with obvious secondary generating characteristics. When the motor began to run wild, it would increase its rotational speed, though this would be fought by the generator mechanism at the core. If the avalanche continued, the rotation would continue to speed up, and eventually the Earth would explode from increased centrifugal stress. But it won't happen. The tap's self-extinguishing in these latitudes — as long as it's inside Earth's magnetic field. A tap at the magnetic pole might create a continuous avalanche."

"They knew that then, too." The archaeologist looked at the engineer solemnly. "They knew that eighty-six hundred years ago. You're not the first, you know."

"I don't think I follow you."

"Pull up a chair. Offer me a cigarette and a seat. Get out the beer if you have any. Call off your men or let 'em keep on without supervision. I've got a story to tell you, and I think you'll be interested."

It was a compliment to the archaeologist's reputation that the engineer obeyed his instructions implicitly. He sent the men along home—it was quartering through the afternoon anyhow.

The seats were canvas chairs, but nearby packing crates made easy footrests. The engineer tossed his guest a pack of cigarettes but packed a pipe for himself after he'd opened the beer. Then he leaned back and waited.

The archaeologist paused for a long minute, lighting a cigarette and making himself comfortable. Then he began:

"It's a long and complicated pattern that shows through as the true history of this planet when you look at the evidence instead of at the rationalizations that have been used to explain *what seemed inexplicable to a race of children that couldn't understand what they saw. Somewhat like the myth of Santa Claus — and even when he recognizes the truth, a child has trouble facing that truth when the evidence overrules his childish beliefs; has trouble not only in accepting the truth, but in accepting the fact that the truth is finer than the fiction, and in no way belittles the fiction.*

"The facts behind our 'Santa Claus' myths of history couldn't be understood until we reached the technologically adult stage where we found out that Earth is an electric motor in space and until we developed for ourselves the solar tap that uses the power of that motor."

The engineer laughed. "Your Santa Claus myths will last a while longer, then," he said "Not even the average scientist accepts the Earth as an electric motor yet. Not even in the face of the discovery of the Van Allen belts which prove it. Not even in the face of anomalies in the Earth's magnetic field which indicate vertical current flowing through the atmosphere. The discrepancies shown are more than one percent; and their instruments are capable of measuring to parts per million — yet they ascribe these measurements to 'experimental error' rather than face up to the fact that there is an armature current continuously flowing in at the poles and out near the equator. Most of it's at an altitude that makes measurement difficult, of course; but the measurements are there, if they'll only read them. I've butted my head against a stone wall on that subject."

The archaeologist returned his smile. *"As one*

stone-wall head-butter to another, then," he said,
"perhaps you'll listen to my story with more of an
open mind than the average."

"Perhaps," said the engineer. "Though the fact
that the human animal stubbornly refuses to accept the evidence of his senses in one area does
not prove that every time he refuses a new postulate it's because he's stubborn."

"Fair enough," said the archaeologist. "But let
me point out a few of the anomalies that dispute
history's fictions and point to the truth. First,
some archaeological remains: the pyramids—
geometrical perfections that appeared on five different continents relatively overnight; and that
appeared in the middle of mud-hut civilizations
that could not possibly have built them. The advanced civilization at Crete that appeared and
disappeared so inexplicably. The records and artifacts that show that beryllium copper was used
by the ancients of Egypt — an alloy that can be
manufactured only with electricity. There are the
jungle-covered buildings and artifacts on the east
slope of the Andes and in Cambodia, possible
only with technological equipment. Those are
only a few.

"Or take the mythologies from any part of this
planet — Greek, Norse, Sumerian, Incan, Mayan,
Aztec, Samoan, Chinese, Indian — they all tell
the same story of creation and the early history of
the human race. So does the Bible. So do most
histories. The details vary, but the patterns of
those details are consistent. They are all, obviously, records of painstaking accuracy — and
impossible. As impossible, perhaps, as the record

a younger child of one of the aboriginal tribes might have made of the first visit of members of a technological civilization who arrived by helicopter.

"Or — there are the Piri Reis maps, aerial surveys estimated to be about seven thousand years old. They contain information about the geography of the polar regions that we did not possess until we checked their accuracy with soundings. They were made when the poles were unglaciated. Or — there is the outline of a jet airfield that is still visible, though only from a height, in South America. There are the coastlines of the continents of Earth that fit together so exactly that it's obvious Earth once had only one continent, centered around her pole. There are the rock records of shifts in the magnetic poles . . ."

"I'll grant your anomalies." The engineer was frankly baffled. "I could probably add a few myself. Now what are you going to do with them? Prove the 'aliens are among us' theme?"

The archaeologist laughed. "Not exactly," he said. "No, I'm going to outline the five major catastrophes that geological evidence indicates, exactly as I think they happened.

"The first catastrophe — the one that destroyed an advanced civilization here eighty-six hundred years ago — was a solar-tap avalanche at the pole. That avalanche short-circuited your sphere-in-sphere capacitor, and increased the rotation of this planet until the land mass split and unbalanced its gyroscopic stability so that it was thrown onto a new axis, and the avalanche was brought within the new magnetic field, and damped. That avalanche put floods of carbon 14 into the atmosphere. I think little survived this catastrophe. The animals that survived mutated into earlier evolutionary forms until there prowled the Earth mammoths and mastodons and saber-toothed tigers . . ."

He paused, and then went on quickly before the engineer could interrupt. "The second catastrophe was man-made, too, but this one was intentional. About 4400 B.C. A melting of the polar caps to cause a flood and torrents of rain — done to wash the atmosphere clear of the carbon 14 remaining from the first catastrophe. During this, because of less-than-perfect planetary engineering, a thousand-foot-high tidal wave swept the animal life from one end of the Earth to the other and deposited crushed bones of animals and humans from cold climates and from equatorial regions alike into piles and caves where they were immediately covered with sand and rubble. There are piles of these crushed bones found in caves a thousand feet up in mountains; and there are hill-high piles of them frozen into the tundra in all the arctic regions — flesh undecayed and still edible when they were found.

"Then there were the catastrophes of near-historic times. The blow-up of Sodom and Gomorrah about 2200 B.C. that created the Dead Sea. And the catastrophe around 1450 B.C., when Earth had become the base of operations on the fifth planet, and the fifth planet blew. In the resulting blast Earth was thrown from her axis again, and from her normal orbit. There is evidence of the planetary engineering done to right her. It took fifty-two years.

"Then, after a long interim, there was the renewed grid-system, and the catastrophe of 776 B.C. when the entire grid blew; when the electrostatic effect of the remaining installations on Mars caused recurring catastrophes for the next two conjunctions with Mars."

The engineer stared at his guest in some dismay. "You sure don't dream small," he said quietly. Then; "Just how do you deduce a series of events like that from the mere existence of the solar tap?"

The archaeologist shook his head. "The solar tap was one of the missing factors. Without it, the pattern didn't make sense. A knowledge of the electromagnetic/physical structure of the planet and the solar system is another. Without that know-how it would be impossible to deduce the causes of the obvious occurrences. Our advances in the biogenetic sciences and in the knowledge of chemical structure are necessary to understanding that which we look at when we look at history. We are only now growing back into the 'knowledges of the Lord.'

"Others have seen that the catastrophes occurred; others have noted that the 'primitives' of antiquity could not have done the things that had obviously been done. But there was no explanation that fitted all the facts.

"But once you know that planetary power exists as an induced current through the molten silicon layer between the core of Earth and its crust, and and as a driving current through the ionosphere, and that it can be tapped and controlled, and what a tap will look like with it is set up — why, then, the pattern begins to come clear. Then you know that that power has been tapped before — the insulators for the taps are standing right there proving it. You know that for it to have been tapped, there had to be a civilization here that had gotten out as far as the Van Allen belts and knew their meaning."

He paused, then went on thoughtfully. "The catastrophes and their dating have been deduced before, but it's taken courage to publish the findings. For instance, Velikovsky outlined the historic and geologic evidence that prove and date the last two catastrophes — the ones in 1450 B.C. and 776 B.C. — in great detail, in 1950. Because the technological know-how was not then developed, he assigned them a specious cause.

"Once you know the basic factors that were at work, you merely have to postulate a civilization here eighty-six hundred years ago that had reached almost exactly the point that our civilization has reached today. Then give it the solar tap. Then take that civilization forward a few dozen years, put a tap at the pole, and avalanche it. That's all."

"That's all?"

The engineer's tone was sarcastic, but the archaeologist ignored that. "They called the Earth 'Atalama' in those days," he said softly. "It's come down as Atlantis. But it wasn't a continent. It was the planet itself. And in those days — about 6600 B.C. by our reckoning—there was only one land mass; a huge, single continent centered around the pole and stretching down toward the equator. It was a Baron Sivos who discovered the solar tap back then, and they called the taps 'Siva generators.' "

The engineer shook his head. "It won't wash," he said. "Of course, Atlantis has been postulated before. But there's one great argument that refutes Atlantis — or your Atalama. A civilization of that high a technological level — or this high — would leave artifacts and lots of them. They'd still be here after eight thousand years, or sixteen thousand for that matter. Kitchen middens of gigantic porportions, if nothing else."

"The artifacts are there." The archaeologist was undaunted. "They don't appear as artifacts until you know the story. Then you begin seeing them for what they are. Will you listen? I think it may be important."

The engineer grinned wryly. This was hardly what he'd expected from a man of the archaeologist's reputation, and he ruefully remembered the men he'd sent home. Then he relaxed. He'd been working hard, and an hour or so spent listening to — well, science fiction — wouldn't hurt him. Probably do the men good, too, to have an unexpected break in the tight schedule they'd been keeping.

"I'll listen," he said.

"I'll start with some detail, then." The archaeologist settled back in his camp chair. "Even after Atalama got the solar tap, it took a while for the economy to adjust to that much power. But they adjusted, and within a dozen years they had switched to broadcast power. With power to waste, you can transmit by broadcast, you know, and simply tune in to it as a power source, the way you tune a radio. Nikola Tesla showed us that could be done back in 1911.

"They had ground effect machines — GEMs, as we do today; flying carpets which ran on the broadcast power and didn't create smog.

"In those days a man didn't get a doctorate, he got a lordorate; or rather, the term used comes through today as 'Lord.' Instead of being known as 'Doctor So-and-So,' he was known as 'Lord So-and-So,' or the early version of the term. 'Baron' probably signified a doctorate in physics, but of that I'm not sure. I'm sure of the lordorate."

"Hold on," said the engineer. "Even if I granted your basic postulate, these are mightly finitè details to be able to specify this much later." If he were going to go along with this, he told himself, at least he'd have some fun out of it.

"It comes through." The archaeologist smiled at his host's expression. "I've been rereading history with a new eye. I never bothered to read the book carefully before, but now I find myself going to bed with the Bible."

"The Bible?"

"The Bible. The story of the Lord of Molecular Biology of the University at Créta, who used the DNA patterns in his own cells to create Adam and Eve — and who created the domestic animals from the undomesticated ones he had in his laboratory, and from the cells of frozen meats he had on hand.

"And the various mythologies and histories —

the stories of the different peoples that influenced eighty-six hundred years of history: the created men; the starship men, the colonies of the returning starships, the miners, and the mutations left from the avalanche — the trolls and dwarves and 'little people,' the fairies and their like.

"It's amazing the amount of detail that comes through, when you look. Even the numbering system, and the names, to some extent." He paused. "Still willing to listen?" he asked finally.

"I'm listening," said the engineer.

The archaeologist leaned back in his camp chair, put his feet on a packing crate, and took a sip of beer.

"The story begins," he said, "in what would be about 6600 B.C. by our reckoning. . . ."

The inaudible electronic whine of broadcast power from the great Siva generators was the pulse-beat of civilization—inaudible except at the sites of the generators themselves where the thunderous, gulp-ended pulse of the ionospheric tap was controlled by man: the broadcast power that was the energy on which he fed.

"Shee-op. Shee-op. Shee-op." the double-pulse beat through the silencer tunnels of the granite pyramids that were the Sivas' insulators. "Shee-op. Shee-op. Shee-op."

It was early evening when that thunderous pulse at Siva Five suddenly became the crash of an unseen fist. A second crash—then silence.

White-faced, the technicians in the control room centered within the pyramid looked to one another, counting their number.

All had been inside.

In the telephone systems leading from Créta to the outside world, the fuses smashed open, then closed again as the surge of power came and went. Auxiliary generators went into operation, replacing the broadcast power with local energy until repairs were made.

In the air, the hellish glow of avalanche lit the dusky skies with a glaring brilliance, then faded. The normal flow of carapet traffic slowed, stopped; the vehicles lighting where they were; the owners fuming, but recognizing the fact that they were stuck.

At the University of Créta, Lord Dade Ellis felt his hair try to stand on end and knew that it meant a ruinous surge of electricity in the atmosphere. Frantically he reached for the switch to the breadboarded receiver, independent of the university power-supply system, with which he was tapping an harmonic of the Siva's base frequency to test his newly built instruments.

Even as he reached, the thin, reedy *eee-op* with which his receiver had been pulsing became a *whap*. He knew he was too late. His work fronted toward the distant generator, and the glare that lit the skies seemed to his dazzled eyes to go on and on, though he knew it could have lasted only a fraction of a second.

He didn't have to glance at his instruments to know that they were ruined. The bleary vision of eyes still blinded by the glare would have made such a glance useless anyhow.

Cursing himself for an idiot that he had not

fused his handmade receiver for such a malfunction at the Siva, he felt his way towards the low-
arched marble hallway beyond his lab. Only secondarily did he realize that the shock wave would
not follow for minutes, since the station was
kilocubits from this spot.

As his vision cleared and he returned to the lab,
a dark gorge of anger suffused him. He stood star-
ing at the months of work that had been termi-
nated by the brief, self-extinguishing avalanche at
the generator.

Dimly he heard the background babble of technicians and professors of the School of Advanced
Study of the University—knowledgeable people,
supposedly. Yet most of them were questioning
what had occurred without using their percep-
tions to arrive at the quick answer he had known
to be correct even as he had felt the surge.

But this time the slight feeling of his superiority
over his fellows only increased his bitter anger at
the frustration of his work in constructing the
now-ruined instruments.

Knowledge that such disasters with the Siva
generators were nearly always put down to 'conditions beyond our control' by the technicians in
charge displeased him even more. This particular
'condition beyond control' he would bring to
light, and the hapless technicians involved would
not be allowed the saving grace of hiding behind
such a stupid phrase.

He strode angrily from the lab, intent on being
among the first to investigate the malfunction.
But in the parking lot he was brought to a second
halt. Here were row upon row of the tiny light-

weight carapets, interspersed occasionally by larger carajets—but, he suddenly realized, all absolutely useless as vehicles of transport until the Siva station was back on the air.

Other people were beginning to gather in the parking area. Some were attempting to start the ground-effect caras with no results. Without broadcast power, they were simply so much deadweight.

The shock wave caught the group—a mighty hand of wind, nearly irresistible in its outward sweep. As he leaned into it he calculated its force—nearly 280 kilocubits per hour.

Behind him in the university buildings, windows swayed and shattered; some of the lighter-weight ornamentation was stripped from the upper levels. Even the majestic gouphra trees lining the driveway and spotting the campus had their great, low limbs swept upward by the blast.

He glanced around at the scene as the wind brushed past—a scene of apparent disaster, with bodies sprawled about and the effluvia of ornamentation and branches scattered widely.

A minute was enough to convince him that no one was badly hurt, and he turned impatiently back towards his lab. Anger had betrayed him to danger as surely as the stupidity of those around him had betrayed them.

A streak of yellowish fur and green eyes, belonging to one of the biological animals—a big one, nearly 40 pounds, and with sharp, deadly teeth and claws—came past him, followed by another animal—110 pounds of great gray muscular fury. Behind this, a few of the biologist's assistants, calling on the animals to halt and calling on the people around to help; though one voice, plainer than the rest, was warning people to say out of the beasts' path.

Suddenly the cat turned in snarling fury and launched itself directly at his enemy, clearing the snapping jaws and coming down, claws out, in a savage attack on the back. The cannus rolled and came back to the attack, but the cat was away again, in a new direction.

Without quite comprehending why, Dade emitted a sharp whistle through his clenched teeth, and directed an automatic command towards the huge cannus. "Come here," he said, and was quite surprised to see the animal break off the pursuit and turn, tail between his legs as though apologizing for having caused so much trouble.

Still with his tail between his legs, the cannus came up to Dade and licked his hand. In reply the engineer reached down and patted the big head, wondering as he did so at his own daring, though the slashing jaws stayed closed, and the cannus stood quietly at his side, trembling under the man's touch.

One of the biology assistants was approaching rather hesitantly, a collar and chain held out of sight of the animal, his other hand out. Dade felt the beast's muscles tense beneath his fingers, the fur at the back of its neck rise.

"Better not." He spoke quietly to the man. "Where does he belong? I think I can take him back there for you."

"Sir—if you would, sir. In the biology lab." The assistant didn't move as they spoke.

"Then move from between us and the lab."
Dade smiled briefly. "Make it slow. No sudden
motions."

When the path was clear, Dade took a slow step
forward. "Come along, boy," he said to the beast at
his side. It moved with him, still trembling but
obedient.

The strange pair walked quietly towards the
building entrance, people clearing the path before
them. When Dade opened the door, the beast still
seemed quite content to accompany him. They
turned at the right of the main door into a long,
bench-lined room with scattered tables and
equipment. Still the beast stayed at his side. Dade
looked around for a clue to where it should go.

"Lord Ellis. The door at the far end of the room,
if you will be so good." Dade had not turned as his
name was spoken; now he moved forward, still
slowly, to the far door, and through it into a
marble-floored room that was empty, save for
quilts that might have been bedding in one corner,
and a feeding trough.

The animal hesitated at the door, but entered on
Dade's command. Almost regretfully he closed
the door upon it. "Good-bye," he said through a
grille, as though to a person, and turned to leave.

A lean figure, almost ascetic, of medium height
and with raven-black hair, was waiting for him.

"I'm David Lyon," the man said. "That was one
of the animals I've developed in the lab, and a very
valuable one. I congratulate you on your courage,
and thank you for capturing him for me."

"Lord Lyon. A pleasure meeting you. But you
knew my name?"

"We all know the engineer who will be in charge of the Vahsaba."

"Not if we have many more of these generator avalanches!" Dade looked around at the cluttered laboratory, gloomy in the half-light of dusk. "Have you a minute to talk? I'd like to find out about this animal."

"If you could make it another time? My babustin is still loose."

As he spoke, the laboratory door through which Dade had first entered opened and the yellowish-furred animal that had attacked the cannus entered as though coming into the throneroom of its palace. Immediately behind the babustin was a young woman in slacks who strode purposefully towards a door at the side of the lab and opened it.

"Into your quarters, Meig," she said, and the big cat stalked disdainfully in, to have the door shut upon her. The girl turned back to the two.

"Got Meig back for you, David. But this— whatever it was—has upset her, and she may be hard to handle for a bit. Do you know what happened, Lord Ellis?"

"Oh, Siva Five avalanched," Dade answered almost casually. "It's wrecked some of my instruments and probably done a deal of damage, but avalanches aren't actually a major catastrophe any more. They're self-extinguishing in these latitudes."

"Professor Zad Shara," Lyon introduced the girl.

"Lord Shara," Dade acknowledged.

"No. I don't have a lordorate. Just professor." She smiled.

"Zad's mentor for the sixth ship, the Vaheva," the biologist put in, "and quite a hand with our high-psi babustins. We've developed them from the bayabs of the province of Philesta. You know, of course, that we are attempting to develop companion animals for the interstellar ships—to act as decoys and guardians for you Vahnire when you reach a planet?" Dade nodded. "These two," the biologist continued, "seem to be among our most successful strains."

"I'd heard the work was going on." Dade looked thoughtfully at the aquiline-featured man before him, noting the coarseness of the hair that grew on his arms; the deep shadow of beard on his face, contrasting with the aesthetic features; the dark cast of the skin. "I had put off finding out about it in the press of other work."

"You really really shouldn't have put it off," Zad said impatiently. "Some of the most exciting work at the school is going on here—and probably some of the most far-reaching research outside of interstellar exploration. Of course, I'm a Vahnire myself and prejudiced in favor of my own job," she said, turning to David Lyon and smiling. "No insult intended. Meig is going with me," she added, turning back to Dade. "She's my own special guardian-companion."

"And what did you have planned for our ship, Lord Lyon?" Dade found himself intrigued. "The animal I just met is magnificent, truly magnificent. And he comes under control at once. Obedient!"

"The cannus is developed from a wolf strain, of the desolately cold regions of Canna. It shows none of the psi characteristics that the babustins exhibit. I have about decided to discard them in favor of the feline strain."

"Do you mean to tell me that the—babustin— can obey an unspoken command?"

"Oh, no!" The biologist seemed genuinely horrified. "Certainly not! Not on two counts. In the first place, the babustins are *not* obedient in the manner of the canines; and in the second place, I said they showed psi *tendencies*, which is a far, far different concept from that of psi communication, or telepathy, which I am afraid exists only in the realm of the public imagination."

Zad put in quickly, "Meig can sense emotions. She can respond to an emotional environment. But she is a completely independent creature, and a very intelligent one. She also retains her full animal capabilities and can hunt and fend for herself. She doesn't need me, any more than I need her. But the two of us make a very good team and can work together well when we want to."

"The cannus is quite the opposite," added David Lyon thoughtfully. "He exhibits the characteristics of a symbiote. He can be independent, but he seems to prefer a partnership with a member of the race of man. The canni that we have tested form a partnership with a man as complete as their ancestors form with their mates—a till-death-do-us-part attachment on the part of the cannus for its master; an obedient subservience toward that one person and no other."

"Now, that would be the animal for me." Dade could feel the big head beneath his hand, the trembling of the muscles in response to his touch.

"I could never tolerate an animal that wasn't obedient. Will they train?"

"The indications are that the person to whom they attach can train them almost to his will. But they exhibit none of the psi qualities, and I am afraid we shall have to discard them."

"You shall not discard an animal of that caliber!" Dade's voice was that of a commander to an underling. "I won't have it! That particular beast, in fact, shall be mine, and I shall take him with me on the Vahsaba." He glared at the biologist who looked back at him in perplexity.

"But Lord Ellis. You do not understand. I am a molecular biologist, charged with . . ."

"And I am the chief engineer of the ship on which a beast is to be placed."

The biologist turned to the girl nervously. "This is a little ridiculous," he said. "I am charged . . ."

On the far side of the door leading to the cannus's compartment there was a low growl; the sound of scratching could be heard against the door.

"I think," Zad said softly eyeing the engineer, "that you may have found a man of the same violent temperament and the same loyalties—and perhaps, if you will forgive me, Lord Ellis, the same lack of psi—that your cannus exhibits. You may, David, have trouble unraveling the attachment, short of killing the one or the other. And I think," she continued softly, "that if you kill the one, you will quite possibly make an implacable enemy of the other."

"Your mentor has analyzed the situation quite well, Lord Lyon," said Dade. "I shall be back to visit my animal. Quite frequently," he added as he turned to the door.

Outside the laboratory he found himself at a loss. Now just why had he carried the thing that far? The beast didn't mean anything to him, although, he admitted to himself, it was a most magnificent beast—and obedient. Obedient to a master, and he was its master!

He smiled grimly to himself, and started towards his lab. Then he hesitated, debating going on to Station Five to see what the damned technicians had discovered in the way of an excuse. He changed his mind again and leaned against the wall beside the laboratory door to wait.

He didn't have long. Zad was only minutes behind him, brushing through the door and down the hall without noticing his presence. He had to take several long strides to catch up to her.

He fell in step and caught her arm. She looked up, and her glance was hesitant and then full.

"Dinner?" he asked. "We could discuss the relative merits of our guardian-companions."

"You were quite rude to a very sensitive scientist," she said severely, and then smiled. "At seven. I'll meet you. At your lab."

"Well . . ." He was nonplused, then shrugged. "Very well. I'm working in room one-seventy. Building Eda."

2

"Once you had the solar tap, of course, you had the stars." The archaeologist was speaking almost wistfully. "Not just the solar system — the stars! With that much power — three times ten to the twentieth watts of continuous energy is your estimate, you said? — you can put as much hardware in orbit as you need to. With real hardware in orbit, their technology — and ours — is quite capable of a stardrive."

The engineer was enjoying the tale. He was relaxed. The sun was westering, and the heat of the day was near spent. The beer was cold, and it was a long time since he'd simply lounged and put his feet up. Stardrive? Sure. With the power you'd get from the solar tap, you could get enough hardware in orbit. Easily. He could design the means himself.

"That's what I've dreamed," he commented. "That's what I hope."

"You won't have to dream. You'll have it. They had it with a technology similar to ours." Ignoring the engineer's obvious disbelief, the archaeologist went on. "By the time they'd had the tap for a few dozen years, they'd managed to launch five interstellar ships. They launched seven in all."

The engineer leaned forward and knocked the dottle out of his pipe. "Now," he said, "even if I take your thesis as gospel — just how could you know something like that? That's a rather far-fetched assumption, isn't it?"

"No. That's recorded fact. You see, the Einstein equations work—and at least five of those starships have made trips back — in what were short periods of time to them, but that represented centuries on Atalama."

The engineer refilled his pipe. "Okay," he said. "Your story includes, as all good science fiction should, the assumption of the inverse ratio of time and matter." He leaned back in his chair, applied a match to the bowl of the pipe, and puffed the tobacco alight.

"Yes," said the archaeologist quietly. "My story assumes that the Einstein equations are real statements of actual fact; that the great Vahs, the interstellar ships that have returned, have proven the equations. . . ."

The ship hung well out from the planet, a tiny snowball in space. The man working over the computation panel in the control room was a tiny entity in the vast snowball of the ship.

Rahn Minos, captain of the Vahsaba, the great starship that would take mankind's Vahnire 2,200 light-years from their home planet, hunched over the ship's computer, his spatulate fingers working the keys carefully. He was checking against penciled notes the complexities from which he was drawing simplicities.

With a gesture of weariness, he threw down the pencil, leaned back, and ran his fingers through heavy brown hair. Then he eased his huge shoulders back against msucles that had begun to ache with tension.

He abruptly shoved his chair back and walked over to the viewscreen that dominated the bridge, the control room of the ship, nestled deep in the heart of its snowball.

Atalama centered the display, its single land-mass uppermost, lapped gently at its furthest edges by the mother sea which covered two-thirds of the planet.

Centering the land mass, almost directly below him, Aetala—the planet's northern pole—seemed a glistening crown on the cloud-flecked greens and greys of the continent of Ura. Around her polar crown, Ura made a slightly lopsided circle, its edges indented with the mouths of rivers and harbors and bays. The lofty peaks of the Laya mountains looked from here like pebbles roughening the continent's smooth surface.

Rahn's eyes traced the outline of the Layas. It was there, high among those forbidding peaks, that the physicist, Baron Sivos, had his laboratories. It was there that he had first discovered the clue to the ionospheric tap—the solar power

source—and had built the first of the great Siva
generators that made the interstellar ships possible.

The ionospheric tap—the solar tap. So simple
that the most backward technology could handle
its construction and put it to use; so sophisticated
that men had had to reach a technology capable of
the laser and of atomic power before it could be
discovered.

With the tap had come power—thousands of
times more electrical energy than man had been
able to manufacture with all his generating stations before its discovery. Power to feed the
world. Power to drive machines. Power to throw
into orbit the heavy blocks of equipment and insu-
lation needed to create a starship and to build an
interstellar drive where it could free itself from
the gravitic field of the planet.

Power to create a technology beyond the
dreams of the puny atomic and hydroelectric stations that had powered men's dreams before.

Yet with the power came its dangers. A malfunction at any of the coastal Sivas caused an
avalanche of proportions that might not be disastrous, but that were both disruptive to the growing broadcast-power economy and disquieting to
the people who used it but still feared it. Such
avalanches were not frequent, but they did occur.

An avalanche at the polar tap would be another
story. The magnetic field of the planet in the
coastal areas near the equator was at right angles
to the magnetic field of the tap, and the interaction of the two extinguished an avalanche; but the
lines of force of the magnetic field at the pole were

nearly perpendicular to the planet—parallel to the tap—and there would be no interaction. If an avalanche occurred there, it would continue to burn, and no one knew what the results might be.

Yet for this same reason the power surges were greater at the poles; the mighty blasts of power needed to throw into orbit the tons of mass needed for the ships were available there as nowhere else. There was the factor, too, that through the polar "hole in the doughnut" of the proton and electron belts trapped in the magnetic field, it was possible to send men and animals without the heavy shielding that would be necessary at any other location.

And so the polar tap had been built, with the most elaborate of safeguards and a constant watch for solar flares that would augment the charge on the ionospheric capacitor and that might instigate an avalanche.

The arguments against the polar tap had been long and bitter. There were many knowledgeable men who still felt that the stars were not worth the gamble. There were more who simply felt an unreasoning fear of the power that all the taps represented. The construction of the polar tap, now more than ten years in the past, had augmented that fear until it had become a growing, restless surge of feeling throughout the mass of the populace, led and fed upon by the increasing displacement of the technologically unable in a civilization that was exploding technologically overnight; and led and fed upon, too, by those who profit from churning the fears of the uninformed.

That public unrest centered on the Sivas as objects of hatred, Rahn knew; and insofar as that hatred centered on the polar tap, it was, he also knew, possibly justified.

He could barely make out, on the planet below him, that huge polar Siva at Aetala, the most powerful of the great generators; potentially the most disastrous, and yet the one that made possible the starship on which he stood: a snowball of polar ice, raised in huge blocks from the polar cap, with the control systems, the crew's quarters, and the huge holds for the 2,000 colonists and their equipment nestled and shielded in its center.

The Vahsaba. The seventh ship, its goal nearly 2,200 light-years out. Nothing short of the tremendous power of the polar Siva generator could have raised the parts for this ship. Megalar by megalar, the great blocks of ice from the polar cap had been raised by the tremendous blasts of power into an orbit in space. Month after month the preformed blocks of ice had been welded and fitted to form the huge central mass of a stardrive ship; a central mass that must be moved far out into space before the dainty spiderweb of plastic could be rigged to her; the dainty web that, spread to nearly planetary size, could be woven to serve as the mass-trap that would power her.

The ice was for shielding, since near the speed of light running into so fragile a piece of energy as a radio wave gives the impression of meeting an enormously powerful X ray. But the ship itself would be the dainty spiderweb, containing this central block of ice much in the manner of a very small spider at the center of a very big web. A

spiderweb of air-rigid plastic film fingers linking
metallic conductors and supporting a structure of
electrostatic deflection and electromagnetic
focusing grids that would sweep a nearly
planetary-size area of space, plucking the few
molecules of hydrogen out of each area that it
passed, and focusing them toward a central reaction area that was only cubits in size.

The magnetic traps would sweep space and
focus in its debris—perhaps only one molecule of
hydrogen per cubic centimeter; perhaps as many
as five, distributed over the area of a whole cubit.
But traveling near the speed of light, that much
mass becomes a density ahead; and that density
would be magnetically trapped and forced, con-
verged into a stream of mass; caused to interact in
a hydrogen fusion reaction, and then thrown
away again, in the manner of a jet airship collect-
ing air at its nose, heating it, and kicking it out at
the tail.

Stardrive. A sweep of the tenuous gases of emp-
tiness into a focus of hellfire and a sweep of that
hellfire backward into a deadly wash that would
drive the ship forward, at first in tiny increments
of motion—but those tiny increments com-
pounded per second per second until, within six
months, the ship would have reached nearly the
velocity of light itself. At that velocity, time is a
relative matter; at that velocity a ship can cross a
galaxy in a matter of weeks ship-time; while on
each planet in the galaxy that same time-span is
measured in centuries.

The calculations must be precise. The ship
must brake, must give up its tremendous energy of

flight and slow itself at the far end of the course. And this was even more complicated, for the particles swept in by the nose must be converted to energy and redirected out through that same nose, slowing the ship down to the relatively low velocities of suns and planets.

Six months to build up speed, while crossing measurable distances; weeks at .98 C to cross distances measurable only in terms of light-years; and then, again, six months to build down to the speeds of mere suns and planets.

And mass, thought Rahn, becomes near infinite; is compacted more and more into a smaller space until its density is such—to the rest of the galaxy—that it is almost invisible; its size is microscopic. Yet was that fact, or was that only observation by the receding planetary observer? Like velocity, mass has been shown to be relative. The theories were exact. The inverse ratio of time and velocity had been proven. Yet—what will the fact be like to a living thing, to a human being on the spaceship? Will the man on the spaceship see, instead, the mass of the system he has left behind compact to infinite density, while he remains the same?

The preceding expeditions had not yet been heard from. Even if any of the first five ships had turned around immediately on reaching its destination, they could not be heard from for Atalaman decades. The interstellar ships—the great Vahs—were not limited in range per trip, other than by considerations of real time. Once they reached their maximum speed, the elapsed ship-time computations were such that they might cross half the galaxy in a matter of months of ship-time, though such a voyage would mean an elapsed time on Atalama of megayears.

Rahn turned his attention to the viewscreen that showed the Vaheva, a tiny bubble reflecting the sun's rays like a crescent moon against the black of space. *She's nearly ready to go,* he thought. In a few days now, her atomic motors would take her to the trojan position, 60° retrograde of Atalama, where she would spend two weeks opening up and fitting her plastic web, like a giant sailing ship unfurling its sails.

And then? By then the Vahsaba would be ready to go, and they in turn would unfurl their plastic sails—their electromagnetic web—to capture the particles of the galactic winds, and to sail the seas of time and of galactic distances.

Rahn tore himself from his reverie. There was work to do before he caught the shuttle back to Atalama. He'd be tied down at Créta for several days, supervising the last details of clearing personnel and equipment, before he could return aboard.

"That's quite a ship you've just described." The engineer leaned back with a quizzical look on his face. "Remarkably well thought out for a storyteller. It reminds me in some of its details of one that was recently written up in a scientific paper. Bussard, I think. . . ."

"Yes," said the archaeologist. "R. W. Bussard's Ram-Jet Vehicle for Interstellar Flight. Published in 1960 first, wasn't it? It's the same research towards the same end—nearly nine thousand years

later. The principles of the utilization of energy don't change much in nine thousand years."

The engineer laughed. "No, they don't change," he said. "If it had happened before, that's probably how it would have been done. But I gather there's more?"

"Yes. There's more." The archaeologist looked across at the engineer for a moment, then out at the dusky desert sky beyond the canopy. "Remember Scheherezade? And the Thousand and One Arabian Nights?" he asked.

"Sure," the engineer answered. "It was one of my favorite kid-time stories. And I'll admit you've got a point there. It could be translated to mean familiarity by the storyteller with a lot of things we know now that couldn't have been known when the stories were first told, or even when they were written down, centuries later. Aircraft, flying carpets, mechanical horses. I think even a mechanical man. And there were the walls that killed when you touched them, and other references that could be translated to mean the use of electricity. I suppose you've got Scheherezade in your story? She'd be a darned good addition, even though I may consider her inclusion rather farfetched. It's a fascinating yarn."

"Yes," said the archaeologist. "Yes, it's a fascinating yarn. I'll grant you that." He stretched and lit another cigarette. "If you'll open me another can of beer, and if you'd like, I'll go on."

The engineer grinned and reached for another can from the small bottled-gas refrigerator at fingertip distance from his seat.

"I reckon I quit believing in fairy tales or science fiction about the time I went out to get my first job. But I still read science fiction, and I've been known to read through my small-fry's books of fairy tales on occasion, just to see if they still hold the old magic. If you don't mind a certain amount of skepticism, I'd like to hear the rest. I'll try to keep an open mind, but. . . ."

The archaeologist laughed. "Fair enough," he said. "And yes, Scheherezade is in my story. It's not her name. 'Shahara' meant 'of those who control the sun.' — but I can't persuade myself to abandon the old title. So I've been calling her . . ."

When Zad Shara reached Dade's lab that night, she was dressed in green silk slacks that fitted at the waist, but hung loose to the ankles, where they were pulled in by slender bands of gold. On her feet were soft gold slippers. Above the slacks she wore a loose gold vest over a white silk shirt. Her hair was tied back with a filmy green kerchief, just out of her eyes, hanging loose, its darkness contrasting with the white of her shirt.

Dade began shucking his lab smock as she opened the door. He looked ruefully at his own white silk shirt and plain gray slacks.

"I'm not fittin' for your garb," he said. "Want I should go change?"

She laughed gaily. "You'll do as is, but there's a party waiting for us, if you don't mind. Rahn and Pacia Minos, and a gang are going to Club Five and have asked us to join. You don't mind partying with your captain, do you? He says there's a new combo at Club Five that's building a reputation as fast as an avalanche—and he said it sounds almost as dangerous."

"I'd better change for something like that."
Dade looked at her solemnly. "I rather enjoy Rahn
and Pacia. Who else?"

"Well . . ." She hesitated. "David Lyon and his
assistant, Memph Luce of Furra. And Captain and
Mrs. Gavarel of my ship. That's all. Really, you're
fine as is. They keep those places so dark that
nobody will know what you're wearing."

It was dark and crowded as they entered Club
Five—a cavernous nightclub. Its single light
came from atop a central pyramid, a model of Siva
Five, from which it took its name.

The two stood at the door a minute, waiting for
their eyes to adjust to the gloom before making
their way between the tables in search of their
friends.

Finally they found them with the aid of a
waiter, ensconced near the stage in a booth designed for eight, but allowing for the eight only by
the utmost squeezing together.

"At least we'll be able to talk to one another,"
Pacia Minos told them, gesturing at the tiny space
into which they were to jam themselves. "If we
can hear ourselves talk. This show had better be
good," she told her husband. "We're sacrificing an
evening's get-together for it."

"It'd better be good because it's probably our
last night on the town in Atalama for about
twenty-two hundred years—and Atalama may
have changed when we get back." Diane Gavarel
smiled happily from beside her quiet blond husband, the captain of the Vaheva.

"I haven't heard that it was *good,*" Rahn told them all. "I've only heard that the songs and feelings that seem to be sweeping all Ura are to be heard here—and that the Vahnire would do well to know what's going on."

Memph Luce gestured to rise when he was introduced but found it impossible in the space. David Lyon greeted Dade without animosity; the engineer was relieved. The man could have taken offense at this afternoon's set-to, but—well, chelt! He wanted that beast!

The music started, a normal enough tune for a normal enough nightclub, even if it was exceptionally dark and cavernous. Dade captured his date for the first dance. As they reached the floor and he swung her lithe body against his own heavy, almost ponderous form, he spoke into her ear. "You look almost as dangerous as that cat of yours."

"Maybe I am," she answered. "This place gives me the creeps."

"Want to leave?"

"Ye gods, no! I've got to find out what's going to happen. The crowd feels keyed up."

"Why you've hardly been able to see the crowd. Unless you mean our own gang?"

She laughed. "No, I don't mean our own gang. I mean the people around us. Look—you may not have been able to see this room very well, but I'll bet you could describe its construction and the system of lighting. Well, I can tell you about the people. It's not only my job, it's where my interest lies."

"Yes, I could tell you how the thing's designed

and lighted with a ninety-five percent accuracy. You're right. That's where my job is and where my interest lies. Tell me about the people. Or rather, tell me about you."

He was only half-listening to her voice as he felt the smoothness of her muscles moving in perfect synchronization with his body. He was clumsy at dancing, he knew, but she made him feel adept.

"The crowd's waiting. I can feel it; or rather I can sense it. They're dancing the stay-apart, jump-up-and-downs on most of the floor, and we're a bit away from the other dancers; but can't you see it? They're not dancing for dancing, they're dancing for interim. And quite a proportion are just sitting, waiting. There must be something really good coming. Well, no—good is not the word. Something really vital. Something they're expecting that's got an internal twist. . . ."

He swung her in an arc away from him and back into his arms, taking the moment to look at her closely. As she followed the motion without effort, her eyes were on his, but intent, unseeing, almost as though she were listening to a distant sound.

The music ended and they made their way back to the table.

"The waiter finally got here. I ordered a drink for you," David Lyon told Zad, rising as she was seated. "And wine for you," he said to Dade. "On Rahn's say-so," he added. "I was afraid we wouldn't get a second chance to order soon."

"You did well," said Dade, seating himself at Zad's right and sampling his drink. "Hmm," he added, "rather good for a club."

"Should be, at the prices." Pacia was on his right, a full-bosomed, full-hipped woman. Her statuesque figure had an appeal just opposite that of the slender litheness of his date. Her rather small mouth and rounded, quite broad shoulders held a promise of vigor, a vitality of emotion that, he decided, could be exciting—if she weren't the captain's wife.

"Should the Vahsaba's ordnance officer be seen drinking in a place like this?" he asked. "Shouldn't you be keeping your head clear in case there are dangerous characters about?"

"I don't think I shall have much worry about seeing to the safety of your supplies," she told him severely. "Unless it's to protect them from beautiful young mentors. I understand you've demanded one of the canni to protect you."

"Have you seen the beasts? They'd serve you as well."

She laughed. "David offered me one. But he did it after he'd noted that perhaps the cannus did fit your personality more adequately, being a less subtle beast than the babustin. So I refused. I think," she said sotto voce, "that mostly I refuse to be insulted by ninnies."

Dade turned his eyes to the biologist sitting beyond Zad, his assistant on his far side. The man's strikingly aquiline features caught his eye as they had that afternoon. He was clean-shaven, but the deep color of his beard showed beneath the skin, contrasting the large, full, overly red lips. He was drawing a diagram of some sort on the tablecloth at the moment, intent, his fingers long and precise, his gestures exact.

"No," said Dade slowly. "Not a ninny. But, I think, a little too—perhaps too intelligent for his own common sense."

At his left, Zad was intent on the biologist's drawing. "You're quite serious, aren't you David, about living on the sea?"

"Quite serious," he told her without looking up. "The work I am doing is leading in unexpected directions. I think if we are where the experiments can be carried out in a closed ecology and without interference, it will be much better."

"And what in molecular biology needs to be guarded—unless, of course, you were indulging in quite inhumane experiments? But no," she added as he looked up in amazement, "it's not in your character."

"No," he told her formally. "That is not—it is very much not—in my character."

"Then," she went on, almost to herself, "let me see. Shall you mind if I guess?"

"I don't promise to admit it if you guess correctly."

"You won't have to," she said. And then abruptly; "It must be quite dangerous—your work—for you to take these precautions."

He nodded. "Quite dangerous," he said. "At least, quite dangerous if it is improperly released. Not otherwise," he added with a quirk of a smile.

"Then I think I shall try very hard to guess. You have," she continued, as though ticking off points on her fingers, "built a submersible ship that is as self-contained as a starship—an improved version of the underseas exploration ship, the

Juhada. That gives you the closed ecology, and the name of your ship—the Juheda. It is financed only in part by the foundation that supports your work, so it is for something you have not told even them of. The ship is to be for the sea, of course, not space; and it contains very little room for its propelling engines, so it's not going to be the voyaging you're especially interested in. I understand that it's three hundred cubits long, a fair length; and fifty cubits broad; and thirty cubits high. So it probably has room for at least three levels of living and working quarters. That's good for a fairly large complement of personnel—but you're not taking many. Twenty is the figure I've heard. And animals, I assume. But that many animals?''

She watched him, and his fingers were slowing in the drawing of the sketch of the Juheda he'd been making. The music started; Rahn leaned forward to ask her to dance, but she shook her head, barely taking her eyes from the biologist.

At her right she felt Dade rise, and from the corner of her eye saw Pacia join him. Across the table the Gavarels rose to dance. On David's far side, his assistant was listening unobtrusively to her words—a strikingly handsome young man, olive-skinned with dark eyes and a quick, flashing smile, and a manner that personalized his slightest remark.

"As far as I've followed your work" she went on slowly, "you've been attempting to strip the DNA in living cells of the interfering chemicals—or to control DNA molecules and—well, the way it was put to me, to bend them to your will. And you did quite a bit of work with the nucleotides. You were working toward cures of the addictive drugs and alcoholism."

The biologist did not look up, and she gazed at him curiously. What could excite this man sufficiently—a self-contained ship; he could—he almost necessarily was—planning to stay out on the sea for years, away from the research facilities at the university. He was possibly planning to get lost until his work was complete, and he did not expect that completion for years. He was in his early forties, perhaps.

She shook her head. "This will take some thinking," she said. "I shan't try to hurry it."

David's head snapped up with what could have been a gesture of relief.

"Much too serious a topic for an evening at Club Five," he said with no attempt at lightness. "Dance?"

She nodded and they left the table.

Rahn Minos leaned back in his chair watching the couples on the dance floor. Lyon and his assistant were still listening intently to Zad, and for the moment he was isolated from the need of being sociable.

Damned good mentor, that Zad. He wished he had her on his ship. But he'd get the benefit of her work, according to the carefully detailed plans. The Vaheva was going just half the distance of the Vahsaba, and, since ship-time would be the same for both—although planet time would be measured in twice the number of hundreds of years for him as for the Vaheva—she should be making her second trip back to Atalama with the Vaheva at the time his ship returned from its first voyage . . . *if* they returned, he added, in the deep distrust that he admitted only to himself.

He trusted the drive; he trusted the formulas. It was only that they—all seven of the interstellar ships and their personnel—were to be the guinea pigs. *Yet I wouldn't trade places with the planetbound if I knew the factors were reversed,* he admitted to himself honestly.

But what did it feel like to travel just under the speed of light? To become so dense that time nearly stopped? According to the theories—and who knew them better than he?—the men to whom it happened had no sense of the happening; and perhaps the new theories that velocities were simply manifestations of angular momentum in time; that the density was a mirage, the time warp the result of the angle—perhaps these would be proven true instead. Whichever was correct, he'd reach the new system in what would be little over six months to him, while on Atalama 2,200 years would have passed.

He watched his wife dancing with Dade. The two were matched, he thought, in size, in— arrogance was a word that sprang to his mind, and though he nearly refused it his honesty forced him to accept it. In size, in arrogance, in animal vitality. That bit about the cannus had been typical of Dade. It would, he thought wryly, have been just as typical of Pacia.

I'm slower, he thought. *I'm much slower. But the things that they miss in their quickness are bred in my bone. I'm awkward where they are graceful, for all their size. But they tread on people, while I use them. They never see the problems they brush through. They never see the people they injure in their passing. Nor would they care if they saw.*

He turned back to the three left at his table in time to see David and Zad rise and make their way to the dance floor. The two couples, he thought, were as opposite as day and night. Dade and Pacia—vital, shining, forceful, irresistible and— uncomprehending. While David and Zad? David saw too much. David's intellectual drive would wreck him in the long run. Hawk-faced to the point of ugliness, lean to the point of emaciation, urgent to the point of driving his body beyond its limits.

And Zad? Rahn watched her critically. That was another question. Another question entirely.

The music stopped, and the light atop the model of Station Five flared briefly bright, and then dimmed. A roll of drums echoed through the cavernous nightclub and ceased into abrupt silence.

The couples on the floor made their way back to the jammed tables almost hurriedly and a hush came over the crowd. Even Pacia and Dade, seating themselves with a start of chatter, quieted suddenly. And into the silence, as though it were being heard only now but had been there all the time, came the slow, deep, almost whispering sound of a drum.

Slow. So slow, so whispered, that he found himself reaching for the sound. And beneath it, on the same note, a single voice, chanting. It was a

full minute before Rahn could recognize the iden-
tity of the word—the sound—of the chant as it
swelled infinitesimally into a full voice. It was the
voice of Siva.

"Shee-op. Shee-op. Shee-op."

The drum quickened and its volume grew until
it was a beating through the room, and the chant
quickened and grew with it.

"Shee-op. Shee-op. Shee-op. Shee-op."

Above the drum in quick fingers of sound a
tomtom, and another voice taking the tomtom
note. "Siva. She-beast. Siva. She-beast."

Then a third voice, high above the first two and
quicker yet. "The power the power the power the
power. Take the stars. Rape the stars. The power
the power the power the power . . ."

The three voices alternated and interwove in an
intricacy of rhythm that laced its way through the
scales, and a wailing chorus in harmonics that
were unharmonic; in clashing dissonances took
up the cry until the room reverberated, while underneath the big drum kept the beat, quickening,
slowing, quickening, slowing, but always with a
rhythm that echoed through his body as though it
were part of his body.

Now the words of the interweaving voices were
changing. "Siva the regenerator Siva the destroyer Siva the regenerator the destroyer the regenerator . . ."

And the high voices. "You love her and you hate
her. She takes your job and you love her and you
hate her. She gives you power and you love her
and you hate her—love her—hate her—love
her—hate her . . ."

While underneath still, "Take the stars, rape the stars, the power the power the power the power . . ."

When the dancers came on in the half-light, they were nearly naked, which was no surprise. But their dance was—primitive. Violent. Based on the rhythm of the tomtoms and as exciting.

Rahn felt sweat breaking out on his forehead. He saw Zad leaning across the table toward him, her hand reaching out to pluck his sleeve. With an effort he pulled himself from the near-hypnotic reach with which he had been listening—not to the chorus but to the deep drum underneath that slowed and quickened and slowed and quickened infinitesimally.

"That drum." Zad spoke with a tense excitement. "That drum underneath. It's taking the rhythm of the heart, and when it slows, you tend to slow your heartbeat; when it quickens, you tend to quicken. You're right," she added. "What's here could be dangerous."

Rahn nodded, grateful.

But why? he thought. Of course, the money being poured into the great Vahs represented a return to the people who stayed behind only in a future so distant that their children's children's children would have been forgotten by then. And, too, the words the chorus had used and then abandoned came back to him: "She takes your job and you love her and you hate her." It was true, of course. The Vahs were creating jobs, but automation was taking them even faster. Was that it?

Now the voices were listing the starships, mouthing their numbered names as though spitting them out. "Vahada, Vaheda, Vahterra, Vahsata, Vahela, Vaheva, Vahsaba. . ."

Then all the intricacies faded into one deep, pulsing, gulping "Shee-op. Shee-op. Shee-op. Shee-op," that went on and on.

He'd heard that the religious fanatics were making much of the occasional avalanches, of the wickedness that they claimed had grown through Ura and that they credited completely to Siva. To "She."

He hadn't thought of the generators as *Siva* before. They were just generators. They were solar taps. They made possible the stars.

But these—these drums and chorus—they were making Siva a being, a force, a person, a god.

Or a devil.

It was dying away now. How long had it lasted? He glanced at his watch and estimated the time since it had started. Half an hour? An hour? Incredible!

And the room was quiet with the absence of the bass drum. It was a quiet as complete as the noise had been before, and it lasted for minutes before the crowd noises began again.

Rahn wiped his forehead with his napkin. "Whew!" he said. "That one was for real."

"Chelt! What an experience!" Luce's handsome head was thrown back, eyes closed, lips parted.

"I almost expect to get lynched," said Dade disgustedly. "I'd expect people to lynch the Vahnire after an orgy like that." He drew a deep breath. "I think," he said, "it's time to go home. That was an emotional wallow, and I need some fresh air."

Zad leaned toward David Lyon, and spoke almost into his ear. "You would be in more danger than the Vahnire if they knew what you had, wouldn't you?" And at his startled guilt, she added, "It's regeneration."

He stood up abruptly. "I wonder if you would come to my laboratory tomorrow afternoon for a conference?" he asked her formally.

She stood up beside him, tiny and graceful. "Yes," she said, turned directly towards him so that her voice could reach only to him. "And I'll keep my mouth shut in the meantime."

3

"Maybe you know," the archaeologist said, cocking an eye at the engineer who was filling his pipe with a preoccupied air. "Maybe you know, being an engineer, about the recent work we've done in this civilization in RNA and DNA research?"

There was a pause before the engineer spoke. "Excuse me," he said, "I was still in that nightclub. Funny, you know. People are reacting that way to automation today, and it wouldn't take much . . ." He shook himself and looked up. "Yes, I've read about the DNA research. It's been widely publicized."

"Then you know," the archaeologist continued, "that the DNA in every cell of your body carries the full pattern for re-creating your body?" The engineer nodded. "And you know that it's been proven theoretically possible to re-create a man from one cell — from his fingertip — or even from his rib."

The engineer nodded again.

"You may not know, though, that the work hasn't stopped there; it's gone much further than the parts that have been released."

The engineer grinned. "Now we get to Adam and Eve," he said, and leaned back contentedly, his pipe going well. The sun was just dipping behind Mount Cholla, and the desert had taken on a golden glow that seemed to bring alive each feature of the arid landscape.

"No," the archaeologist interrupted his thoughts. "Not for nearly six hundred years yet. At the time of my story, though, the work in DNA and RNA had reached just about the point that the unpublicized portion has today. The lord of molecular biology at Créta was one of the foremost in that work. . . ."

Zad arrived at David's lab shortly before lunchtime, hardly expecting him to be in yet since this was Heladay. Four days of the week the labs were normally busy from early till late; but the fifth day—the final day of the week—most of the scientists stayed away from the campus, at least until afternoon.

She hadn't slept a great deal the night before. She'd been almost rude to Dade, preoccupied, wishing only to get to her own quarters as quickly as possible where she might think.

She was intensely excited. Her own academically disapproved and strictly side work with the memory tap toward extending the human life-period and amplifying the ability potential had seemed to be making tremendous strides. She hadn't thought of the possibility that the same goal could be reached chemically.

She could recognize David's need for secrecy. Chemical alteration of the life-functions was something done to a subject, and whether it were with or without consent, the public outcry would be great against the doer if anything went awry.

Work in the memory tap hadn't necessitated such secrecy. Any life-extension or improvement achieved by the memory tap was the result of hard work that the subject did himself; hard and fairly frightening work for the subject. Dangerous in its way, but done of, by and for himself, and hardly conducive to catapulting an entire populace into any longevity worth worrying about—far too onerous and frightening to the subject himself to be actually dangerous to humanity. And, if he were less than competent in his handling of the memory tap, the subject was apt to null—whether temporarily or permanently hadn't yet been proven—even his own normal human effective-ness, so he certainly posed no personal threat to humanity.

But chemically achieved release of the re-generative factors of the human body? When un-controlled, that was cancer of course. And if David had only partial control, he'd be subject to lynching expeditions if the work became broadly known.

As she approached the biology building, she

saw David's carapet in the parking lot and quickened her step. The still clarity of the bright day, the campus empty of students—quiet, civilized, manicured—brought a surge of content through her senses; content to be identified in the sometimes ambiguous but always urgent striving toward higher goals; the refusal of man to be thwarted by his own limitations, whether those limitations were imposed by factors of the life around him, or were self-contained—the beast within.

She tapped gently on the laboratory door before entering, and David's voice bid her a gruff "come in."

He had evidently been working on some papers, but he dropped them with a rather grim smile. "I couldn't sleep, so I came down early. I didn't really expect you before afternoon. Coffee?" he asked.

"Where do you keep the makings? I'll fix it." Zad walked down the aisles between the laboratory benches to the corner toward which he had nodded. "I couldn't sleep, either; but I waited until now thinking you wouldn't be here."

David came over to where she was heating the pot.

"What worries me mostly," he said, leaning against a table nearby, "is that since you caught on so quickly to what I'm doing, others may catch on too. When I show you my early results, you'll recognize the need for its not being known until I've gotten it under far better control."

Zad kept her eyes on measuring out the coffee. "I don't think that need worry you, really. We've been doing work in much the same direction with

the memory tap. Too bad we haven't gotten together before this. It could be our work is supple-
mentary to yours, or vice versa. You are going to
tell me how you're going about the work, now that
I've guessed the direction your results are taking
you, aren't you?"

"Oh, yes," he said casually. "Of course. Anyhow, you're a scientist and will recognize experimental beginnings and differentiate them
from actual, usable, releasable results. Of course
I'm going to tell you—and leave it to your own
common sense to keep it to yourself. Anyhow,
you'll be leaving the planet in—how soon now?"

"Three weeks, till our scheduled takeoff for retrograde orbit. Barring holds, of course. We'll be
two weeks in the trojan position, unfurling our
sails—but nearly out of communication. So effec-
tively it's three weeks."

The coffee was ready, and the two made their
way to an uncluttered area of a bench, pulling up
lab stools.

"Suppose," said David, "that I start at the beginning and outline how the work is done. Then
I'll show you some of our results. You know the
work we did in isolating DNA as the pattern-
carrying part of the cell? We were able to show
without question that the DNA in any single cell
of the body carries the pattern for the entire body.
It was widely publicized and popularized. Fairly
accurately, too."

Zad nodded. She'd read of the work. A popular
magazine had even given the story nearly an entire issue—including its cover.

"Of course, once we had the pattern-carrying

function isolated, we knew it would be possible to grow a man from any single cell. We also knew— and this wasn't publicized—how to go about recovering the regenerative process that the body contains—the process that's shown partially when the body heals its wounds; the process that is seen in the ability of, for instance, the starfish or the planarian worm, to regrow its full body from any part of that body.

"You see, the DNA which is in the nucleus of the cells in man and animal and on down to plant life, carries the entire pattern for the body in which it is contained. But those parts of the pattern that will not be used by the unit cell are covered up so that each cell *won't* reproduce the entire body. Also, the DNA has a system by which it determines when to stop reproducing cells for its own particular part, once the person is grown to full size. This signal lies in the autonomic nervous system in the human, and is closely connected with the development of the glands at puberty.

"However, even after it receives the signal—for instance, when the liver has reached full size and receives the signal that its cells need not keep on producing liver cells anymore—the repair system functions to give the signal for reproduction of cells back to the DNA specifically affected when the body is injured, or even just as the cells wear out and need replacement.

"Now at a point in the development of the human, the cells and body parts quit reproducing themselves as they wear out, or produce less efficiently—and that's when aging begins.

"Of course that's the point we've been working on hardest—the loss by the body of the ability to maintain itself in youthful condition. It's an ability we all have during early maturity but that we lose later. The loss of that continuous regenerative ability is the aging factor. And that is the area in which I'm getting answers.

"But the answers are too good. The methods we've tried so far that return to the body its regenerative ability go all the way back to the beginning and start the cells to reproducing whole extra arms, or livers, or heads. We haven't got it under control yet. And you can see the kind of problems that gives us, if somebody should make a complaint.

"And—well, the animals we've treated aren't killable, by any normal method. Injure them, and they regrow the part, surprisingly rapidly. But they're just as apt to go ahead and grow another head, for instance, at the same time."

"And they're really not killable?"

"No. That's the part that's astounded me most. Injure them in a vital organ—the heart, for example—they go into a cataleptic condition and appear to be completely dead; but thirty-six hours later they're right back in business, just as if nothing had happened. During the regenerative cataleptic condition they become anaerobic as well. They can't be smothered or gassed."

Zad stared in awe. Then; "Population explosion, here we come—when you get this under control!" she said.

"Not necessarily. There seems to be some interference with the reproductive capacity. It's not definite yet. Perhaps they will both work together; perhaps they won't. So far, we've noticed that there is interference. The one seems to be exclusive of the other.

"But—well, when you release the regenerative faculty, there's no way of disposing of the mistakes. The bodies won't die, that is, short of burning the entire body to a cinder. The regenerative faculty works—too well, in this case. You can see my problem.

"Of course, the major problem is that the methods we've developed for releasing the regenerative faculty leave it unselective. There doesn't seem to be any natural handle in the chemistry we've developed so far. You know that the fetus goes through the entire evolutionary process in reproduction? Well, the regenerative factor is just as apt to pick out an early evolutionary characteristic to regenerate as a recent one. For instance, one mammal developed fins. Sometimes there's an increase in the animal's mental capacity; but just as often it's apt to redevelop a type of mental process suitable to survival in one of the earlier evolutionary periods. . . ."

Zad looked up, startled. "Hey!" she said. "That's one of the major problems we've found in using the memory tap! Quite a number—a small minority, but a respectable minority—change physical characteristics toward an earlier evolutionary period through the use of the tap. Nothing as dramatic as you've outlined, but very definite. The mental characteristics are apt to change dras-

tically as well. Mostly for the better, but in a statis-
tically respectable number of cases, for the worse."

Lyon stood up in a quick motion. "You mean
something like that has been going on right under
my nose, and I didn't know of it? What is this
memory tap, and in which building are you working?"

"Oh, no—not here at the university. The work
is in very great academic disfavor. But I consider it
of even more far-reaching importance than the
solar tap."

Lyon sat down again, slowly. "All right," he
said. "What is the memory tap?"

"Oh. You know that the electronic brain is the
input area for information in the biochemical/
electronic configuration that is man. And that the
electronic input information is evaluated by the
intelligence and then filed biochemically in the
cells of the body. The electronic input and ana-
lytical system is far faster than the biochemical
data-storage system, so that the body has to sleep
while the data-filing system catches up with the
input and analysis.

"Once filed, the information is utilized without
further review. Now, under certain conditions—
notably, during periods of great pain, uncon-
sciousness, or hypnosis, the incoming data is filed
without analysis, and its content is apt to be rather
badly misfiled on an "I" equals "eye" sort of basis.
Misfiled information can become a glut of
stimulus-response command-data within the
body and can be quite detrimental.

"The memory tap is simply a method for recalling misfiled information for review and analysis, and then for refiling correctly."

Lyon drew a deep breath. "Very well," he said slowly. "I am academically shocked when you speak of electronic-input and a biochemical filing system for information. I had assumed that the brain had the information-carrying function."

Zad laughed. "The brain is on an electronic data-bit-per-cell basis. Not enough capacity for one week's information input. Biochemical data storage is another matter. Your DNA can carry the entire evolutionary pattern of man in one part of just the nucleus of the cell."

Lord Lyon went on as though he hadn't heard her. "I also find it quite difficult to believe that any work which is academically refuted can carry any basic importance. And I find it quite difficult to associate 'misfiled information' with stimulus-response reactions. However, I respect both your ability and your scientific integrity. And therefore I demand a complete briefing on this subject."

Zad looked at him curiously and restrained the laugh that bubbled to her lips. How typical of the man! He would fight to the last ditch to refute any evidence she produced, but he was so basically honest that he was one of the few in the physical sciences she was sure would not simply throw out the evidence when he found he could not refute it.

"David," she said, "I'd be delighted to brief you myself. But it will take time, and we're leaving in three weeks. But I shall send you my best man, Bon Hindra. And if you do not take him with you on your—what is it, a ship or a boat?—your submersible, I shall admit that I've misjudged you. For the sake of both sciences, we'd better get together. Now about your work?"

"Oh, there's not much more that I can tell you until we get a bit further. Except to ask that you protect me by silence until I'm gone. I'll show you my mistakes if you like."

"Never mind," she said, recognizing the deep pain in his voice. "You know I won't talk. We'll let the rest go until your research is complete. But I'll send you my man Bon and you'll listen to him. I rather think that if you do, you'll take him with you."

"What makes you think he'd go?" Lyon's voice showed the relief he felt.

"We're working toward the same thing you are, from a different direction. Bon and I have been working together, and when I leave he'll have to start a new project, though he'll stay in the same field, of course. Your Juheda sounds like the spot for him."

"Well, I'd rather have you brief me, selfishly; and I wish I thought I could tempt you to stay planet-bound and come along on the Juheda. But I shall appreciate his briefing and listen carefully. Now, since I'm not going to show you my failures, would you care to see the ship?"

"I'd love it." She stood up. "Where do you keep it?"

"In the Bay of Carria. But that's only an hour from here, and we can lunch aboard. I've a crew in residence, and we're completely stocked, ready to leave as soon as I've completed my work with the animals for the Vahs."

"Did you ever read the Book of Revelations in the Bible?" the archaeologist broke off to ask.

The engineer was caught in one thought sequence, and he took a full minute to switch to the new one. "I've skimmed through it. I couldn't make any sense out of it. It sounds—well, like a man on hashish. For instance, it's talking along about the guy on the horse that has the power to bring peace, and suddenly it says 'A measure of wheat for a penny, and three measures of barley for a penny, and see thou hurt not the oil and the wine . . .' "

The archaeologist laughed. "I think that bit was illustrating the advent of the traders in the sequence showing those who came to try to make this planet a colonial outpost of empire." At the engineer's questioning look, he continued, "Suppose you showed an aboriginal tribesman a cartoon training film on how to handle epidemics? Or an educational TV film on history? You've seen the type of training film they use in the armed services? And the kind of background-taken-for-granted visual education films they use for students. Try showing them to a complete primitive, one who doesn't even know that such a thing as civilization exists and who thinks you came down from heaven on a magic carpet. And then you ask him to record exactly what he's seen in those movies in his own words, and to preserve the record and not let anybody change a word of it.

"Try rereading the Book of Revelations as a

series of such movie scripts. I'm ahead of my story, but suppose somebody very loyal to the Lord wanted to carry out the promises he'd made, and did the best he could to carry them out. Then, when he had to leave, about 60 A.D., tried to leave the best record possible in the hope that it would last through to the time when people could understand the message.

"So suppose he took his brightest primitive, John the Apostle, and showed him a batch of training films illustrating all that had happened in sixty-seven hundred years, and illustrating also how to handle things like epidemics and radiation? Remember, this is a primitive. And the primitive sees the people on the screen as real, rather than as pictured. And the primitive follows his instructions and writes down exactly what he believes he saw, and ends with the strong admonition that no word of what he writes is to be changed.

"If you reread the Book of Revelations as a series of training-film scenarios translated through the eyes of a primitive, it comes through. . . ."

It was not long after noon when Lord Lyon and Zad left the lab, and the campus, though still quiet, now had a few figures under its giant trees, strolling between its buildings.

As they entered the parking lot and made their way towards David's carapet, Zad heard a halloo, and the two turned to see Rahn Minos just parking in the next row.

"Where are you going so bright and early?" he asked as he strode over to them. "I thought we kept you up late enough last night to make you both skip work entirely today."

Zad smiled delightedly up at Rahn, one of her favorites of the expeditions. "We *are* skipping work," she said. "We just decided to play hookey this afternoon."

"We're going out to see my new ship. It's finished and stocked, you know, and I expect I'll be taking off before you do." David was almost gay in the bright Heladay atmosphere.

"Hey," said Rahn. "I've heard of the Juheda and I'd like very much to see it. Will you take me out there some day?"

"Why don't you join us now?" Zad felt a quick surprise at the obvious pleasure with which David offered the invitation, for an invitation to view the Juheda was known to be hard come by; then she realized that David had as much respect and affection for the big man who captained the Vahsaba as she had.

"Let me take you in my carajet." Rahn was obviously pleased. "I'd be delighted. I feel like hookey too, after last night. I'm not really expected here today, anyhow. Just came down to get rid of the taste from last night."

The carajet was a fairly large one, and they raised ground as a GEM for only a few minutes' travel before taking to the airways and heading south.

From above, the mighty Ura River by which the University at Créta nestled seemed to meander across the verdant plain as casually as a tossed lariat. In the distance they could make out Siva Five and the scorched land around the great pyramid where yesterday's avalanche had churned the landscape for nearly a kilocubit. No major damage had been reported from the malfunction. All personnel had been inside, and as far as anyone knew, the wrecking of what the newscasters termed minor electronic equipment—how that phrase must have rankled in Dade's ears!—had been the worst result. Even the shock wave had done only minor damage.

As they drew near the bay, the long finger of dock where the Juheda was tethered came into view; and the ship herself, a floating bubble of plastic, glinting in the sunshine, two-fifths of her width in height.

"But won't she be at the mercy of the winds with a bubble that large?" Rahn asked speculatively. "I don't think I'd want to take to the open sea in anything as exposed to the wind and wave action as your ship appears to be. In space, of course, it's different," he added, remembering the spherical and much larger shape of his own ship.

David laughed. "No," he said. "Neither would I. Trust myself to a surface craft with quite so much exposed surface. But she's submersible, and we shall ride out any storms at thirty cubits."

"You're pressure-locked, then?"

"Oh, yes. Sealed and pressure-locked with a self-sustaining ecology like your own. And with a pumping system that puts sand into her tanks to take her down. She doesn't need to be an iron monster like her earlier prototype, the Juhada, at nearly sea-weight in construction materials. She can weigh herself down to the finest balance with sand, then pump in water to take herself down as necessary, discarding the weight to rise. Rather like a queen rising out of the deep. I've test-dived her," he said almost shyly. "She handles like a goddess."

"She looks like the kind of fairy bubbles that I used to blow with soap," Zad said almost reverently. "Fragile. As though she'd fly off at a breath of air. She's truly beautiful."

On the dock as they approached her, the Juheda was still beautiful, still light, still awesome. Her hull was clear, and though there was some distortion, the inside could be seen as a shadowy honeycomb of walls.

They entered through a huge freight-tube-lock at her top, that extended down through the four cubits of double hull. A hallway led through corridors lined with hydroponic gardens on the far side of again-clear plastic walls. Beneath the clear plastic at their feet was sand; it felt as though they walked on a plastic-covered beach. A roaring sound, nearly inaudible, could be felt almost as much as heard.

"The sand is being pumped into the space of her double hull," David explained. "We pumped her clear after the test dive, for final inspection. Now she's being filled to a specific gravity just under one. It leaves her barely awash. So if you seem to feel her sinking, don't worry. Now let's have lunch, and then I'll tour you from stem to stern."

He led them into a spacious cafeteria, lined with hydroponic plants and set about with small tables. The far wall of the room was covered with a large screen. Leaving them at a table near the center of the room, David poked his head into what was apparently the kitchen area, ordered lunch, then turned back.

"While we're waiting, let me show you some of the finest teaching equipment you can imagine," he called, and going to a door at the opposite end of the dining room from the screen, he rolled out a white movie projector of the caliber that would be used in a theater, its seven lenses in a half-circle at its front proclaiming it a color projector of the most elaborate type. It rolled on a frame on which it stood on four legs; a rather oblong, rounded body, with the projector forming a head.

"It looks rather like Mary's little lamb, ready to go to school now," Z-n ' said. "A seven-eyed lamb. What a beauty!"

"Technicolor and Vista-vis:on," David said, indicating the tremendous screen. "And stereophonic sound."

"How on Ura did you acquire equipment like the Juheda and that movie apparatus!" Rahn exclaimed. "Your grants must be the most liberal known to scientific history!"

"Ah," David said proudly, "This is only partially from research funds. Haven't you heard that I went commercial? I had some research funds that could be allocated to the Juheda, of course, but they weren't nearly sufficient. So I began commercializing. I've sold books and articles. I even wrote some science fiction—with sound scientific bases, I might add. Two were bought for the movies. And I've been making films for the educational TV channels. I've just been signed by the Knight Interests to make a series of cartoon-films on biology which will be used on commercial channels."

He chuckled as he ran the lead on a filmstrip through the maze of cogs and clips under the projector's soft white cover. "I've even been given two of the Knight Interest's top technicians and this equipment to take with me on the trip. I plan to make films of everything we do, of course."

Zad and Rahn both looked at the biologist in complete awe. "I think," said Zad solemnly, "that I shall sign up for one of your classes—not to learn molecular biology, but to learn the gentle art of commercial success in science."

"What I'm going to show you," said David, disregarding her comment, "is the opening sequence of a new series, and then one of the cartoons. The one we did on radiation is among my favorites," he added, "even though it is rather out of date."

Leaving the projector, he went around the room drawing drapes that covered the entire wall surfaces, creating a theater atmosphere in the big cafeteria. "This room," he said, "doubles as dining hall, theater, and classroom. We'll use the Juheda as a seagoing school after we finish this work.

"You realize," he added, "that in going commercial I have also had to be somewhat grandiose and a bit—well, folksy."

The music came up in a blare of trumpets with a background chorus, and the screen cleared to show David in the tremendous proportions of Vistavision, seated at his desk. Around him was the zodiacal circle in the vivid colors of the highly technical art of the movie. In the place of each sign of the zodiac were two technicians in white laboratory smocks, a Bunsen burner or a crucible beside each as he worked at some task.

At each of the four major inner points of the zodiacal circle was a figure illustrating one of the four branches of biology: a lion, a calf, an eagle, and a prehistoric man. Behind each of the four was the head of a seven-lensed color camera, recording its movements, and each of the four moved restlessly.

Before the desk was the huge lens of a microscope. At the front of the desk were replicas of the seven interstellar ships, their frosted ice lighted from within as from the great stardrives of such ships.

"Hello, hello, hello," said the screen David. "This is the study of biology—the story of all creation that is written in the planet around us and in the stars in our galaxy. The book of life is an open book, open to him who has eyes to see and ears to hear."

As he spoke, the outer part of the zodiacal wheel turned and moved beneath the camera to become a circle at the base of the picture while the lens of the microscope that had been at the base moved before the four biological specimens, enlarging them. Each of the four made its normal hunting sound: the eagle screamed, the lion roared; the lamb bleated, and the man made grunting, presymbolic noises.

Then the lens faded and the animals in their turn slowly revolved into their place in the zodiacal ring which now lay at the foot of the scene, while a white movie projector rolled up beside David at his desk, a duplicate of the one David was using now. From a pile of seven cans of film at his right, the screen-David selected a film and placed it in the projector.

From the Bunsen burners and the contents of their crucibles smoke rose to obscure the scene as the trumpets blared again. The chorus completed its theme while an announcer's voice declared, "The study of biology—the study of life. The study of what was and is and is to be."

The picture flicked off and David switched on lights. "That's the opening sequence for each of the films," he said in his own voice again. "What do you think of it—for commercial appeal that is? We're competing with all the guff the TV is spewing forth," he added apologetically. "We've tried to give it enough drama to catch at least a good part of the normal prime-time audience."

Rahn's voice held nothing but admiration. "I'd say it's rather terrific. It's dramatic, but what's the harm in that?"

"Rahn's right." Zad's voice was enthusiastic. "But what do the Knight Interests get out of it?"

"Prestige. Status. Institutional advertising. Identification with basic research will go a long way toward canceling out their robber-baron reputation. They don't need to advertise their products anymore, just their trade name; but they do need to keep their public image gleaming. This does that without seeming to be commercial."

The kitchen door opened and a food tray was wheeled into the room.

"Lunch is ready," said David. "But while it's being served, let me show the cartoon figures we drew for a radiation sequence. Then I'll be good and leave my toy and eat." He flicked off the lights again, and speeded the film through the projector. A few unidentifiable sequences flashed by, and then he slowed the projector down as a vast army of tiny cartoon figures came on the screen. The miniature, animated shapes were ferocious— with faces like a woman's, teeth like lions', scales like iron breastplates, and tails like scorpions'. Each figure was glowing with internal radiation.

A shout of laughter greeted him as he stopped the projector and flicked on the lights.

"So that's what a gamma ray looks like!" Zad said as she caught her breath.

"They live up to their looks in the script, too," David said proudly. "They torture people by stinging them, but it takes five months to die, and it's a mighty battle. In the long run, they're routed."

Zad and Rahn were still laughing. "David, that's good," said Rahn.

"Anybody that loves cartoons, and that includes me, knows they've got to be gory. Cat smashes mouse, mouse is smashed flat until he un-flats. People will eat that up," said Zad.

Lunch was hilarious, and by the time the three had toured the Juheda from top to bottom of its three levels, examined its atomic motors ("Why not broadcast-power?" asked Zad. "I may be too far down to get it during storms when I need it most," David told her) the day was far spent.

As they left the dock it was already dusk, and the passing circular carapets had switched on their riding lights. In the gathering twilight, the six round "feet" that circled the rim of each carapet rather like glowing upside-down megaphones, and the more powerful central foot cast a burnished light from the motors onto the ground beneath; while the seven riding lights that duplicated their positions topsides looked like tiny fireflies hovering in the air. Through the round, clear-plastic bodies of the vehicles, the figures of their occupants could just be made out.

"They look so dainty and fairy-like," Zad said softly. "If you couldn't hear the motors, you could almost believe in fairyland."

"I'm not sure that what we have now is not fairyland," David told her solemnly. "We've got the power of genies, and we're breaking through to so many secret, magic knowledges. I wonder if we're capable of handling all that's in our hands these days. It takes gentleness to protect the magic of fairyland," he said quietly.

4

The archaeologist broke off suddenly and stood up, stretching. He wandered to the edge of the canopy and stood looking up at the desert stars beginning to twinkle through the dusk. Then he turned again to the engineer.

"We know the Juheda was at sea when the avalanche occurred," he said. "Lord Lyon may just have gone to sea as he planned, but I rather imagine he left hastily—that his work was uncovered and the public raised a hue and cry."

"Are you sure his name wasn't Noah? There's a great flood in every mythology. And the avalanche you're setting up would have caused floods." The engineer's skepticism was unalloyed, but he was enjoying the logic of the build-up.

"No." The archaeologist was quite positive. "No. Noah's flood was later. It was caused purposefully, and it didn't happen until 4400 B.C. The crew of the Vaheva helped Lord David create the flood, the first time they came back.

"But Lord Lyon was underseas when the big avalanche occurred, and he was in a plastic ark of similar dimensions to those he gave Noah before the 4400 B.C. flood. It's 'the bubble in the sea of chaos' by which most mythologies date the beginning. The few exceptions to that story of the beginning are the mythologies where man came from the skies.

"So Lord Lyon was underseas. He may just have gone to sea in the routine course of events, but I rather imagine . . ."

As Rahn put the carajet down in the university parking lot an hour later, two figures were taking off from near the biology lab, with the whirling streams of fire over their heads that indicated the use of the uncomfortable, back-strap heli-jets.

"Darned if I can see why anybody would want to ride on one of those things." Zad seemed genuinely puzzled.

"Oh, they're not so bad. Beat the parking problem as easily as a bicycle, and with a lot more get up and scat." Rahn spoke almost offhandedly. "Pacia and Dade both have them. I think they get about as much kick out of riding the darned things as one of those ski enthusiasts gets from jumping over snowbanks up in the Layas."

"We're taking some along on the Juheda." David stretched his lean figure out of the seat.

"They stow easily and provide transportation when you dock. Come on in the lab for coffee," he suggested, helping Zad out.

The three strolled across the quiet campus towards the big biology building, savoring the serenity of the scene and the feeling of content that had grown among them.

David opened the door to the lab and was gesturing them in, when suddenly he froze.

Barring their way, hands clenched, face white, was Memph Luce.

At the sight of Lord Lyon, Luce's hands unclenched and he let out his breath with a sigh of relief.

"What on Ura . . ." David's voice was completely startled.

"We had two . . . visitors." Luce's voice was high with strain. "I found them when I came in. They were in the experimental section, David."

"The . . . damn! Who?" The biologist's voice was suddenly fierce.

"Dade Ellis and Pacia. Your wife, captain." Luce spoke to Rahn.

"Pacia?" Rahn was puzzled.

"I—I threw them out, David. I had to be—quite ungentle about it. They . . . talked of going to the civil authorities, and took off by heli-jet."

"We saw them leave," Zad interpolated quietly.

Rahn interrupted rather brusquely. "What would Pacia and Dade be doing in the biology lab in the first place, and why would they threaten to go to civil authorities in the second? It—well, it doesn't seem quite in character. Even if you were rude, they had no right to be here."

David seemed not to have heard. "How long had they been here before you found them?"

"I gather quite some time. They seemed to be familiar with every . . . every . . ."

Zad said abruptly, "I think this is a matter between you two. Perhaps Rahn and I had better leave. Or perhaps Rahn, as captain of the Vahsaba, could be of some help to you, if you'd care to make matters clear enough so that it would be possible."

David turned to his assistant. "How serious were their threats? How serious did they sound?"

"They sounded quite serious. Quite, quite serious. And from their attitudes I would think so, too."

"If I can be of any help," Rahn interjected, "I'd be glad to, though I can't think that Dade and Pacia would go to authority for anything so idiotic as being thrown out of where they didn't belong. Dade is rather short-tempered, and perhaps that was just his temper speaking. He's apt to be over his tantrums as quickly as they appear."

"I think perhaps we had better call on your assistance, Rahn." David hesitated, and then said fiercely, "An experimental laboratory can be quite shocking to a layman who does not understand what work is going on. We do not," he said with deep emphasis, "indulge here in inhumane experiments—but we've had some rather unfortunate results from some of the means we've tried—unfortunate and unexpected. I think a man of Dade's character—and perhaps your wife as well—might misunderstand what they saw, and perhaps feel impelled to take action against what would appear to them . . ." His voice trailed off despairingly.

"I see. Yes, if he thought something untoward was going on, Dade—and Pacia, too—would be apt to take direct action. But what could have brought them here in the first place?"

"The cannus." Zad's voice was positive. "Dade is completely enamored of the beast. He and David had quite a row about it."

"Oh. Yes. Pacia mentioned it. Well, I shall see them each. Pacia tonight, Dade first thing in the morning. Put your mind at rest, David. I know you well enough to know that whatever you are doing is all right. I'll forestall any actions they might take. The captain of the ship does have a bit of authority," he added wryly.

"I'll show you what upset them if you like?"

"No need at all. I know you rather well, and I'm not a bit worried about whatever is being done under your authority. I'll tend to those two—and I've got to get on to my desk. There's a mountain of work waiting. Thanks for showing me the Juheda. It was a treat."

"Thank you for taking care of this rather— unfortunate occurrence."

Zad turned to the biologist. "Why not make a night of it, David? Come along to my place, and we'll get hold of Bon now. I want you two to meet, and if you're leaving soon it had better be right away. Would you like to come too, Memph?" She turned to the younger man. "You'll be quite interested in what we're doing with the memory tap, and Bon's going to outline the work for the biology department."

Luce was still pale, but he was making an effort to pull himself together. "Thank you, but I think not," he said. "I rather think someone had better be here, and I've a bit of work to do." His eyes looked haunted.

David took Zad's arm. "If you can get your man tonight, that will suit me exactly," he said. "I'm skeptical, but I shan't want to leave without knowing your work."

"Where do you get this memory-tap business? I know we have the memory tap in its early stages today; but I've never seen a reference to it in history or mythology." The engineer was fascinated with the wealth of detail in the yarn.

"Oh, the memory tap comes down quite clearly on several lines. Through Bon's work after he left David, probably in a quarrel over methodology, you'll find a rather distorted version of it in the Karma concept today; and even the biologist used it in his work to re-create the race of man he thought had been exterminated. You'll find references to it all through the Old Testament, instructions on how to control the 'beast within.' They were rather complete, those instructions, originally; but most of them have been lost. You see, about 50 B.C. it was decided that the work of weeding out mutations and breeding the race true had to end; measures were taken to cancel out the system of burnt offerings and the memory tap and to substitute a system of ethics."

"You insist on those mutations?"

"Oh, there were mutations. Almost one hundred percent at first. The animals that have

been found crushed with human bones and pot-
tery shards in caves a thousand feet above sea
level; and in frozen piles several hundred feet
high in the arctic regions as a result of the tidal
wave that happened when the flood conditions
were stopped too fast — they're almost all throwbacks. Mammoths, mastodons, saber-toothed tigers — throwbacks. It was a major anomaly in the
evolutionary dating sequence. Much too recent,
the bones much too fresh, to match our ideas of
when such animals roamed the earth. The race
the biologist created were throwbacks, too; but
that was due more to the creative techniques than
the mutation hazard, against which he protected
them as much as possible.

"But when he had to put his people out of the
Juheda into the Guarded Area so that they could
have the reproductive faculty without introduc-
ing its chemistry into his closed ecology — they
did mutate. Badly. The record of his work to weed
out the mutation factors is quite complete. The
first incident occurs in the Cain and Abel sequence. You remember that Cain brought the
'fruits of the ground' as an offering to the Lord?
And the Lord 'had not respect' for Cain's offering?
While Abel brought meats, and the Lord 'had respect to them.' The carbon 14 in the atmosphere
wasn't immediately lethal; there was simply too
large a proportion of carbon 14 instead of carbon
12 in the carbon dioxide content of the atmosphere, and I gather the body could handle it in the
concentrations in which it existed. But it was a
genetic hazard—even more to the plants than
animals, since the plants reproduce faster; and

even more to the animals than man.

"The Lord was probably quite distressed to see how badly the plants were mutating, quite possibly making them inedible and poisonous. Edible plants are delicate and mutate easily. The edible strain of potatoes, for instance, is a close cousin or a descendant of the deadly nightshade. Tomatoes were long thought to be poisonous, and probably were; our new edible varieties just came into existence through mutation some time in the last few hundred years. Many of the other vegetables we eat are closely associated with generally poisonous species — even such innocent plants as carrots and parsley.

"When Cain and Abel brought their offerings, the Lord was distressed at the mutating plants, probably found them poisonous, and forbade his children to eat them. But the animals, though mutated, were edible. Of course, the children misunderstood. I gather Cain thought the Lord loved his brother better than himself, a typical childish reaction. Abel may have thought so, too. At any rate, it led to the first murder.

"Then later the means Lord David used to breed out hemophilia comes through quite clearly. The bargain he made with his people that each male child would be circumcised by the time he was eight days old was one of the most binding of his rulings. There was no way he could eliminate hemophilia from the female carriers, who don't develop it themselves; but by circumcision he would eliminate it from the males. Any boy-child hemophiliac bled to death when he was circumcised.

"Incidentally, it's fascinating to note that in the Old Testament, the word 'sin' or 'evil' translates as 'sick' or 'diseased.' The word 'holy' translates as 'healthy.' "

"Now just where," the engineer demanded, "to start at the beginning, do you get enough carbon 14 to br a major genetic threat? To require a catastrophe like the flood or the conditions you describe?"

"Take an electrical discharge of sufficient intensity to upset the balance of the planet. Feed that discharge-arc through a predominantly nitrogen atmosphere. You get carbon 14 and lots of it. Remember, that arc continued for seven days."

"And the carbon 14 would still be sufficient to be a major genetic threat except for your flood." The engineer nodded in admiration. "You've certainly worked this out to the last detail."

"I have simply looked for the evidence — and refused to discredit the evidence, geological and historical, that is to be found throughout the planet," said the archaeologist dryly. "The biologist told his children that they would grow into the knowledges of the Lord. It's about time we grew up and took a look at the evidence and did just that."

"Score!" said the engineer. "Okay," he added. "The evidence makes good listening. What happens next?"

The archaeologist smiled. Even for a man who credited his own senses in defiance of the traditionalists, and was determined to prove the theories behind the solar tap — even for him, such a complete new look at history was difficult, he *thought, and felt a deep weariness. Would the human race ever grow up? Ever quit clinging to preconceived notions in the belief that those notions represented security? Stubbornly determined that Santa Claus must come down the chimney; refusing to recognize the love behind the myth as sufficient security to make it possible to discard the myth? But the child must grow up now! His voice took on a gentleness, a quiet.*

"As I said, Lord David may just have been underseas according to his scheduled plans, when the avalanche occurred. But it is just as probable . . ."

It was after midnight, and Zad, David, and Bon were deep into the details of the work of the memory tap. David was not only convinced, he was becoming more excited by the moment with the manner in which this work could supplement and dovetail with his own. Coffee cups sat around, and the air was blue with smoke.

The phone at Zad's elbow suddenly took up its customarily insistent ring. Puzzled, she answered.

It was Memph Luce's voice, strained but unemotional. "Professor Shara," he said formally, "can you tell me where to find Lord David Lyon?"

"Of course. He's right here." Zad was about to take the receiver from her ear to hand it to David when she heard Luce's voice continuing.

"I am so sorry to bother you at this hour, but I wonder whether you would undertake to locate Lord David for me. Tell him that government officials are at the laboratory now and would like to question him. I am being detained for questioning myself, and the laboratory animals have been impounded. They tried to find Lord David at his quarters, but he wasn't there, and they feel it quite important that they find him immediately."

Zad caught her breath, trying to assimilate the underlying meaning of what Memph was saying. "Of course," she said. "Are you at the laboratory now?"

"No. I have been taken to the police station, and will be held here for questioning. I gather for some time," he added dryly. "I stood on my rights as a civilian to be allowed one phone call to my superior or lawyer. Please tell Lord David that the officials will expect him at the laboratory."

"Is there any more that you can say?"

"No. No, that is all. Just see if you can locate him and let him know that he is expected. Of course, if he has . . . already gone on a . . . trip, it is too late to reach him." Abruptly, Memph hung up.

Zad turned to the other two, paling. "David! Dade and Pacia didn't wait until morning. That was Memph. Your laboratory's been impounded, the officials are looking for you, and Memph has been arrested. That's not how he put it," she added lamely, sinking back in her chair.

There was absolute silence, not one of the three moving, until suddenly Zad sprung up.

"Memph said they'd looked for you at your quarters. He sounded strained, of course, but he was trying to tell me much more than he could say over the telephone. They were undoubtedly monitoring his call, for he called from police headquarters. David! They'll probably come here looking for you!"

David raised his head, his deep eyes hollowed. "What can I do?" he whispered. "What can I do?"

"How near ready is the Juheda?" Zad's voice was fierce.

"Nearly. There's not much—there's not much that's not aboard that I'd have to have, except the personnel."

"Take off!" It was a command, not a suggestion. "Just before he hung up, Memph said that if you'd already gone on a trip, it would be too late to reach you. David, get as many of your gang together as you can and take off. Now. Tonight."

"I'd be—I'd be stopped. I couldn't get them all together. Maybe the investigation won't be too serious. Maybe I can make them understand . . . ." The biologist pulled himself together. "You're right," he said firmly. "I'll be completely stopped unless I can leave before they . . . any publicity would bring out the regeneration factors and people would fight for premature release . . . those who didn't understand. . . . Yes, I'll be completely stopped unless I can leave before they take me in for questioning. But Memph . . . ?"

"You'll have to leave him behind. But I'll get him out, somehow, and hide him—somehow. . . . Anyway, that's what he was trying to tell me over the phone. For you to leave. Right now."

"I'll have to get my people together."

"David." It was Bon speaking for the first time. "I'm going with you, if you'll have me. Give me a list of your people and let me contact them, get as many aboard as possible. How long do you suppose we have?"

"Not five more minutes, if you stay here. That was a pretty broad hint that Memph gave me, and it won't take the police long to tumble. Take David to your place, Bon, and do what's necessary from there. They won't connect you with this. I'll stay here and lead them astray when they come looking. They're bound to come here."

Zad was at the door, impatiently ready to let them out. David reached her side, then stopped.

"Oh," he said. "The ultrasonic separator. It's still at the lab."

"Where is it and what does it look like?"

"It's on a bench at the left of my desk. It's a small black box. About the size of a portable typewriter."

"I'll get it if I can, and I'll get it to the Juheda by dawn." Zad's voice sounded more positive than she felt. "You'd better leave before sunrise. They'll think of the Juheda sooner or later. If they don't know of it now, they will by the time they've talked to a few people. That gives you less than six hours, you two."

David started to open the door, Bon behind him, but suddenly Zad gestured them back. "Reconnoiter," she said, went to the window and peered out. "There's a police carajet just landing," she called over her shoulder. "David, you stay behind Bon—let him lead the way. Go out the back. You may have to walk. They're in the parking lot."

"No." Bon was getting into stride now. "David, you go out the back way and go over to—to the back of the electronics building yonder. Keep in the shadows. I'll go out the front way to the parking lot, get my carapet and take off in another direction. Then I'll circle back and pick you up. But stay out of sight."

"Good boy." Zad was delighted and beginning to enjoy the situation for all its dangers. "Meantime, I'll lead 'em on a chase of some sort. Now, scat. Fast. They're coming."

The door closed behind the two men, and Zad turned out the lights, then watched from the window until she could see Bon nearing the parking lot, while two uniformed figures, having passed him, headed toward her building.

She let herself out of her apartment quickly, down the hall to the front entrance, and out. Ignoring the approaching uniformed figures, she strode purposefully, and as fast as she could without appearing to run, at an angle towards the biology lab.

Out of the corner of her eye she saw the two figures hesitate. Then one turned to follow her; the other continued toward her building. Satisfied, she forced more speed into her legs, still keeping below the pace that would appear to be a run.

"Professor Shara?"

She pretended not to hear the voice. She was nearing the biology building now, and she broke into a run. Throwing open the main door as though forcing her way through a barricade, she turned into the lab at her right.

A guard just inside the lab door stopped her. She glared up at him.

"I understand you have impounded the biology

laboratory and its animals," she told him fiercely. "I have come for my personal equipment and for my personal animal."

"You'll have to get a permit." The guard stood squarely before her.

"At least I shall check to see whether my babustin is being mistreated!" Zad's figure, though small, could take on a good deal of dignity and authority, and she gave it the full treatment, as she walked deliberately around the guard. He reached a hand toward her shoulder to check her movement, but a haughty glance stopped him, and she made her way past, striding toward the door that led to the babustin's cage.

She had reached the door before the guard caught his breath and she pulled it open without heeding his command to stop. Seizing the collar and chain that hung beside the door, she spoke to the big cat that stretched lazily as it approached her.

"Meig! Here!" She slipped the collar over the huge cat's neck, and turned to face both the guard who had stood at the door, and the official who had followed her, who was just entering.

"This is my animal." She spoke as though no question had been raised. "That equipment," and she pointed to the black box that lay on a bench beside the main desk in the room, "was loaned by my department to Lord Lyon. I do not know what question has been raised in respect to his department, but I do not intend to have my own work slowed down by official impertinence."

As she spoke, followed by Meig on her leash, Zad made her way quickly to the box and picked it up. "If you would like a receipt," she continued, moving directly towards the two who stood between her and the exit, "I shall be glad to sign anything that you have in mind."

The newly arrived official smiled briefly, rather as though the smile was painful.

"Professor Shara," he said, "we have no intention of interfering with anyone's work, not even that of the biology department. However, we have impounded . . ."

Zad continued directly towards him. "You have not impounded *my* department nor its property." She had nearly reached them, but they didn't move.

"I am sorry, but—"

"Meig!" Zad spoke sharply, giving a flick of the leash towards the two guards.

Meig launched herself without warning, a snarl that was near a roar in her throat, claws bared. Both guards threw themselves from her path, and Zad was through the opening, Meig turning behind her and continuing to snarl as she kept pace with the girl.

"Stop or I'll shoot the beast!" The voice behind was shut off as the door slammed. Without pause, Zad pushed through the front entrance, and ran to the big gouphra tree nearby. Scrambling up its low branches, Meig beside her, she crouched just above head height as the two officials catapulted out the front door and stopped to scan the empty campus, silent under the star-filled sky.

"You go back and guard that damned lab," one of the figures barked. "I'll circle the building."

The instant the two figures were out of sight, the

one back into the building, the other around its corner, Zad, with Meig, slid lithely from the tree, ran to the next building, and then made her way cautiously through the back areas of the campus to its border, the farthest from the parking lot.

I'll have to find a phone, she thought. *A cab would be dangerous. But . . . yes, Rahn.*

5

"The cannus and the babustin." The engineer stretched and filled his pipe again, settling back. "I understand that you mean a cat and a dog, but why the fancy names?"

"Haven't you ever wondered at the basic difference between the wild and the domestic animals? That the domestic animal seldom goes successfully wild, and that the wild animal seldom domesticates? The cat and the dog were preavalanche experiments in developing companion animals, and very successful ones. But they were not made on the Juheda. They were preavalanche and went with the ships; and only the last two ships, at that. Their first real appearance on Earth is in Egypt for the cat; at Crete for the dog.

"The ancestors of the cats, the entire feline

strain that we know as lions and tigers and cheetahs, et cetera, the animals from which Lyon developed the cat, survived the avalanche on Earth, wild; as did the wolf-family, the ancestors of the dogs. But the dogs and the cats themselves came back with the Vaheva and the Vahsaba.

"There were further experiments and developments in the cats that were first brought back by the Vaheva. A number of animals showed the psi tendency, and work was done to see how far the intelligence could be developed. But especially with the cats. The whole sphinx and cat mythology — the cat-bodied people of Egypt — stems from that. There are indications that cross-strains with the human form were successfully tried on various animal lines, though if they were tried they proved genetically unstable, for there is no evidence that any of the strains survived for more than a few hundred years. It is possible that the mythologies of human-animal crosses are a development from the use of psi-able animals as monitors; but it seems more probable that some of the crosses were temporarily viable, and that instances of the cat-bodied, the bull-bodied, the hawk-headed actually existed; that a satyr, a centaur and others really lived for a brief span.

"At any rate, we know that someone who had worked with the molecular biologist returned with the Vaheva, and remained when Lord David left. We've called him Memph Luce of Furra, and his story links back into that of the Lord and his chosen people.

"But the indications are that later someone else took over the work that Luce was doing, and took it in directions other than those in which it was first initiated. The whole story of animal worship stems not from Luce, but from that other, I think; the story of Ba'al and the like. And Lord David's fury at the results when he came back in 2200 B.C. must have been something apocryphal. That's when he selected out Abraham and his tribe from the descendants of those who had survived the flood, who were now scattered across the planet. That's when Sodom and Gomorrah were blown up.

"At the time of Abraham, you have three types of animals: the wild animals, the domestic animals, and the animals in which, obviously, are represented induced mutations, around which religions were built probably in order to support the work of the laboratories and to handle the care and feeding of the delicate mutations. These last disappear shortly after 2200 B.C., and may be presumed to have been genetically unstable. The religions built around the induced mutations lingered for centuries — there are still traces of them — but the mutations themselves disappeared.

"But notice the domestic animals — the cow, the horse, and the sheep, for instance. Lyon developed those aboard the Juheda — probably created them from cells from meat he had aboard — then bred them for domesticity to serve his people. And whereas the induced mutations did not stabilize, Lyon's domestic animals, developed from cells and selectively bred, did stabilize and survive.

"Notice, too, that the civilization, at the time

the returning Vahnire of the starships built the pyramids and made broadcast power available, went from mud huts to stone buildings, although the existence of Bessemer hearth furnaces then shows that steel was manufactured. Broadcast power would resonate with the steel skeletons of today's structures unless very carefully handled."

"It's not fair," said the engineer petulantly, "to make fairy stories — or mythology — sound true."

The series of phone calls from Bon's apartment consisted of brief, implicit instructions, giving no time to the parties at the other end for foolish questions. The Juheda was leaving at dawn. If they wished to be aboard, they would report there by that time, fully equipped, and as unobtrusively as possible, making sure they were not followed. Under no circumstances were they to go near the biology building, or do anything to call official attention to their movements.

What the extent of the police inquiry would actually be was a matter for guesswork, in these predawn hours, because they could not be sure what Dade and Pacia might have said, nor what force they might have placed behind their arguments. But in every case it was made clear that there would be no coming back, no second chance, for those that might be left behind. The Juheda was one of the few ships quite capable of disappearing into Atalama's vast ocean and remaining hidden indefinitely. The plan was to do just that.

Submersible ships—submarines, some called them—had never been of any practical or commercial importance, their uses limited to the scientific exploration of the sea; so there was relatively little chance of pursuit if they could get under way. Since the launching site was in another governmental district, it was also improbable that communication would be fast enough between the bureaucratic divisions to halt a surprise launching. However, should they be stopped, anyone aboard would be vulnerable to a charge of attempting to thwart a governmental investigation, and it was explained to each that the decision was his own.

There was one possibility that Bon foresaw only at the last moment—that of an all-points bulletin for David himself. Bon decided, "Best we stay right here until the last possible moment; leave it to those aboard to prepare the ship to be ready to leave the minute you make your appearance." One more phone call took care of that, and then the two turned to scavenging Bon's apartment for whatever it afforded that might be useful.

The first streaks of light were just touching the skies when, with everything that either could think of as needed from his living quarters loaded into his carapet, Bon switched on the motor. David, an unaccustomed hat pulled low over his face, came from the building to join him.

Atalama seemed hauntingly peaceful as they flew south. The rosy fingers of dawn touched the night sky caressingly; mist shrouded most of the ground below, and the animosities of mankind seemed almost inconceivable. David found himself wondering briefly whether he were not being over hasty. The thought was quenched in the facts that underlay his flight, even as it formed.

The ocean covered half the horizon now, and nearly beneath them was the bay, the dock at which the Juheda nestled barely awash just visible in the clearing mists—and on a course toward the dock, nearing it rapidly, three unmistakably marked police carajets that could more than match their own speed.

Bon pointed silently and pointed as well toward the open freight lock of the Juheda.

"Will the lock take the carapet?" he asked with biting fierceness. At David's nod, he said, "I'm not going to land. I'm going to take her straight in. There may be shooting," he added as an afterthought.

Rahn's carajet had made short work of delivering the black box aboard the Juheda. Now he and Zad ate breakfast in a windowed café overlooking the dock where the big bubble lay awash. The babustin they had left in the parked carajet, seemingly content.

The flow of arrivals at the dock had attracted some notice, but it had been so unobtrusive that the two could hope the notice was only local and wouldn't reach official ears—not for hours yet, anyhow. They'd told those aboard where they would be, but had left and come to breakfast to be in an advantageous spot should trouble develop.

"We could lead another wild-goose chase, if it's necessary," Zad had said. "I don't know just how we'd manage it, but if we're where we can see what's needed, we can figure something out."

But nothing untoward had occurred that they

could see. In the dark it was impossible to tell who had gone aboard and who had not. David might be aboard, or he might not; and they had no way of knowing.

It was just as dawn began to brighten through the windows that they saw the big police carajets land. Instantly they were on their feet and out the door, Rahn flinging a bill on the counter as he left.

Uniformed figures began tumbling from the police carajets, and without discussion the two headed on a path to intercept the figures, watching as they did the carapet that swooped in above the police, heading for the lock of the Juheda, making the bare clearance as though it were a daily ritual.

Running, Rahn and Zad gained a position between the police figures and the big lock that was slowly swinging closed.

"Clear the way! We're going to have to shoot!" a policeman bellowed at them.

The two turned as though not comprehending, directly in the line of fire to the lock. Rahn quickly shoved Zad behind him. "They'll recognize you," he whispered fiercely.

It was all the time that the Juheda had needed. Already the bubble was sinking, the lock closed, the water closing above it.

"Stand clear!"

But the bubble was gone, as though it had indeed been a fairy bubble.

"I—I'm sorry. I didn't realize—" Rahn turned so that his big body sheltered Zad from view. He took her arm. "Come, my dear," he said clearly. "There seems to be some trouble here. We had better clear out of the way as the officer suggests."

And the two walked to Rahn's waiting carajet, as though hurrying to obey orders. Meig snarled tentatively as Rahn opened the door, but quieted instantly at a word from Zad.

Neither of the two spoke again until the carajet had cleared the area. They could see the big police vehicles hovering over the bay, but by now, they knew, the Juheda had the depth she needed and would be on her way to the open sea.

"Whew!" said Zad at last. "That was close."

"Dade," said Rahn through clenched teeth. "And Pacia." Then he shook his head as though to clear it. "And I gather that you're involved now to the point that you'll probably be summoned for indefinite inquiries if they can find you. Perhaps I'd better take you straight to Aetala. You can go aboard the Vaheva, and stay until take off. You can get somebody to gather together whatever you'll need, can't you?"

"Yes, except for one more detail." Zad's humor was coming back now that the danger to the Juheda was past. "There's Memph Luce, you know. He can't go with the Juheda now, and that gives me the opportunity to take him with me on the Vaheva. I've got to both get him out and get him out of sight, and the Vaheva will solve both problems—if I can get him out. The work they're doing on the Juheda," she said earnestly, "is— well, I can tell you now they're gone. You ought to know, anyhow. They've got regeneration nearly in tow. Eternal life," she added slowly. "Eternal. Regeneration. The works. No more aging.

"We'll be gone a long number of Atalama

years," she added. "When—and if—we get back, civilization will have changed. I want to take Memph with us. He knows the work. Sometimes I think he's more excited about it than David is. We may need that knowledge, where we're going. And you *should* store knowledge of that sort in at least two places."

Rahn guided the carapet quietly. "Regeneration," he said slowly at last. "So that's it. But what upset Dade and Pacia to such an extent?"

"They didn't know—David didn't know—what he had. And, well, some of their experimental animals can't be killed. They're alive but unalive. They're undead. Then there were one or two rather unhappy and quite unexpected results— regeneration of parts of the body that already existed. An extra head. An extra leg or so. That sort of thing. Enough to set an unimaginative, didactic sort . . . forgive me, Rahn. I forgot I was speaking of your wife."

Rahn shook his head. "Don't try to protect me from that part," he said. "I'm trying to understand. I cannot understand Pacia's point of view, but I shall try. As for Dade . . . well, he's the engineer of my ship, and at this late date I don't think I could change engineers. Even if I could, I doubt if I could find his equal in his particular field. But I do not have to feel sympathy with him as a person—only as a member of my officers' complement for whom I am responsible."

He turned a face so drawn with misery towards Zad that she bit back an exclamation. Instead, she said tentatively, "What shall we do about Memph?"

"I'll have to get him out of course. Can you arrange it with Gavarel that he can be taken aboard the Vaheva?"

"Yes," she said. "That I can arrange."

"Then suppose I take you to the Gavarels' quarters now. Then I'll go pull a little rank and get Memph free. After that, I'd suggest the two of you get aboard the Vaheva as rapidly as possible, and stay aboard until takeoff."

The engineer grinned. "All right," he said. "You've got Gavarel — Gabriel? — aboard the Vaheva. And you've got Luce of Furra — Lucifer, I presume? — aboard the Vaheva. And he's a sort of Rudolph Valentino character with an experimental twist which he'll use to upset the normal evolutionary patterns with no end of freak combinations to everybody's intense annoyance. And Captain Gavarel's got all sorts of electronic apparatus that could pass for a flaming sword to put at the gate of the Vaheva when he tosses Luce the hell out of there — to the Vahela? It's an intriguing yarn, to say the least."

"Yes," said the archaeologist. "Yes. An intriguing yarn. To say the least. And of course Luce was the one David Lyon left in charge of the experiment much later, after the flood, when David went off with the Vaheva, taking Enoch and his family to plant the seed on a new planet. It was when the Vaheva came back, in 2200 B.C., that David found out about the animal worship, found his people being used as servants and brutalized, found that hemophilia had been introduced from another planet — and assumed that it was all

*Luce's doing. And he and Gavarel . . . Yes. Yes,
quite definitely an intriguing yarn. . . ."*

The Vaheva had left for its trojan orbit, abruptly
and somewhat earlier than its schedule called for;
and amidst pressure from authorities for the return of the fugitives, Memph Luce of Furra and his
accomplice, Professor Zad Shara. The Vaheva had
unfurled her sails—strung out her magnetic
web—and was even now tacking slowly to the
position where she could turn on the full power of
her stardrive.

Formal complaints had been filed away on
Atalama in government archives, a gratuitous gesture against the possible future return of these
criminals, expectable only in distant centuries.
The governmental attitude and action detracted
from the event of the starship launch, but seemed
to meet with the approval of the public, growing
more outspoken daily, that decried the spaceships and the technology whose culmination they
represented.

The Vahsaba had reached completion, and all
but a few of its personnel, all but the final install-
ments of its equipment, were on board. The last
load of persons and equipment was to be shuttled
up this evening from the huge polar Siva generator
that had been used to launch, piecemeal, the parts of
all seven of the interstellar Vahs.

In his laboratory at the university, Dade Ellis
was working furiously against the deadline, seeing to the packaging of the last of the new instruments to be taken aboard. Official demands for
lengthy testimony on his charges against the biol-

ogy department had taken his time to the point of
frustration; and he had only been freed of an official summons requiring his presence at a trial that
actually postdated his own scheduled departure
by the premature departure of the Vaheva. Like
many before him, Dade was discovering that he
who calls on the assistance of the law quite often
finds himself caught in its toils.

The testimony and the summons were compli-
cations he had not foreseen in his hasty denunciation of the work in David's lab, a denunciation he
now, ruefully, regretted—but without the means
of expression of that regret. After all, David was
the man responsible for his cannus, and even that
had been put in danger by his hasty action.

But the cannus he must have, and that immediately, he decided. He'd tried to get it freed to
him through official channels and had been refused, politely but firmly. But . . .

After all, he reflected as he saw to the last box
leaving on the transport to Aetala, Zad had gotten
her animal free; perhaps he could do the same,
even though the lab was still impounded and
under guard.

Leaving his now-empty laboratory, Dade made
his way hastily over to the biology lab. The guard
knew him by sight, knew him as the man the top
brass had depended on in this investigation, and
did not bar his way as he entered. But as he approached the cage at the rear of the lab, the guard
called out, "Careful with those beasts, Lord."

"Oh, sure," Dade said casually over his shoulder, and opened the cannus' door. The big beast
shambled forth and stood uncertainly, looking

from the man he knew as master to the guard he assumed was the enemy.

The guard was hesitantly reaching for his weapon. "Please, Lord, if you can, put him back in his cage. He's dangerous."

"Oh, nothing to worry about. He's quite harmless for all his looks. I just wanted to tell him good-bye." Slowly Dade and the big cannus together made their way toward the center of the lab. "There's some special food here that he's extremely fond of," Dade explained and he walked obliquely toward a cabinet near the door.

Too late, the guard became alarmed, and the hesitant hand drew forth the weapon. With a low growl, the cannus charged, his slashing jaws tearing at the man's throat as his massive body bore the guard to the floor.

Horrified, Dade commanded, entreated, and even pulled at the great head. The cannus came slowly back from his victim, but it was too late. The guard lay dead at their feet in a pool of blood, the big beast who had slain him shivering under the touch of his master, trembling at the instinct of obedience that withdrew him from his quarry even as that quarry lay fresh-killed.

Trembling himself at the results of his actions, Dade looked around. Except for the body of the guard, the place was empty. The cannus stood now at his side.

Dade hesitated only a few instants longer; then, the animal beside him, he turned and left the lab, closing the door quietly. In the dusk the odd pair made their way to the parking lot and took off for Aetala.

The shuttle would leave in six hours. Dade hoped it would be soon enough.

The carajet hovered briefly, made its short dash slightly above ground level, and took to the air, heading north along the sunset line over the vast expanse of snowfields that claimed a full third of the center of the continent. Irrationally, Dade was pushing the machine to its utmost in a race against the moment when the laboratory would be entered again, its ghastly contents discovered.

The better part of common sense would have been to abandon the beast, he knew. Except for his possession of the animal, there was no clue that would connect him to the dead body.

Yet he had no intention of leaving the cannus behind.

The shadow of time struck farther and farther around the globe; the carajet shortened and shortened the distance to the massive and, at the moment, silent polar Siva generator and the nearby launching field; and as yet there was no hint on the official radio channels of anything wrong. His deed had not yet been discovered. Now, if he could get the cannus aboard the shuttle without being observed . . .

Breaking regulations for private craft, he settled the carajet into the narrow space between the equipment warehouse docks and the shuttle. The questions were immediate, over the radio. He took a necessary moment soothing official upset by explaining that he was saving precious moments by landing here to stow some equipment he'd brought with him. He added nonchalantly that he would remove his craft very soon.

Then, carefully, he and the cannus made their way into the stowage hold of the shuttle.

Working against time, Dade shuffled and re-stacked crates in such a way as to make a carefully concealed hollow big enough to cage the beast; and after it had reluctantly entered, closed the opening with more crates, and realized that he was just in time as he heard voice of the loading crew coming up the gangplank.

Stepping to the entrance, Dade glowered at the approaching men. "These crates," he said. "Even imbeciles could do a better job of stowing. You, there. Take my carajet off to the proper area. The rest of you bring the crates to the entrance. I'll stow them myself."

The loading foreman was taken aback to be thus addressed, even by Lord Ellis, chief engineer. But he wasn't foolish enough to question the order.

6

"If you grant the postulates of this 'intriguing yarn . . . ' " The archaeologist reached for his beer and sipped it a minute before continuing, and the engineer noted with surprise that the hand that held the beer was shaking. "Even if you grant the postulates, then, still, some of the detail may be guesswork. But there are five things we can know: that Atalama had already launched six starships; that the seventh was in orbit, ready for launching, its final shuttle being thrown up to it by the polar tap; that David Lyon was already underseas in his plastic ark, with his equipment; that there was a solar flare — a real granddaddy of a solar flare — possibly because the Vaheva went onto full star-drive too soon, and the backwash of directed radiation reached the sun at that point.

"And," he added slowly, "it can be postulated that there was a technician who hesitated for the fatal fraction of a minute to pull a switch. . . ."

It was hours later, and Dade had at last sealed the hold containing his equipment and taken his place with the rest of the crew in the somewhat cramped passenger quarters of the shuttle. The video broadcast channel, tuned in for their entertainment during the trip, was suddenly interrupted by a news commentator, telling of a discovery just made at the "infamous laboratory of the fugitive molecular biologist, Lord David Lyon." One of the animals, the commentator declared, had escaped, slain a guard, and was now at large. All persons in the area of the University at Créta were warned to be on the lookout for the raging beast, to take cover on sight, and to notify the police instantly.

Dade sighed with relief, even as the voice of the news commentator was replaced by the cold voice of the launching monitor. "Fasten your seat belts, please. Take off will be five minutes from my mark . . . Mark."

There was a scramble of last-minute passengers for the remaining seats, and then the somewhat unreal period of merely sitting and waiting. Worry nagged at Dade's mind. Had he stacked the crates properly? Would his caged cannus be able to knock apart the construction if he took fright during takeoff and in flight?

The minutes faded to seconds. "Ten, nine, eight . . ." the familiar chant carried down from the early rocketeers rang hollowly through the passenger section of the shuttle. "Four, three, two, one. . . . "

The mighty electro/ionic engines came to life, as there was a glare from the huge polar Siva station.

Sluggishly, then majestically, the shuttle began to rise, gathering momentum.

But solar observatories were even now recording another phenomenon. A sudden brightening in the photosphere of the sun. A bulge. And millions upon millions of tons of ionized gases hurtling upward from the photosphere in the incandescent fury of a solar flare.

An astronomer reached for the open communications line to the seven Siva stations.

"Shut down all stations," he barked. "A solar flare is in progress."

In the base of the great polar pyramid, the technician in charge blanched and grabbed the mike.

"Polar station," he shouted. "We can't shut down. We just launched the shuttle."

"Bring them back. You *must* shut down."

"They've already reached the halfway point in velocity," the controller's voice was nearly sobbing. "It would take longer to bring them down now than to keep them going. And I can't cut the power! That would be murder!"

Ion by ion, the charge in the ionosphere increased. Volt by volt, it built upward under the ultraviolet glare from the newly active sun. Second by second, the beam current increased from the polar tap.

A new voice, obviously hastily summoned from somewhere, came over the open line. The shuttle was in its last seconds of powered flight.

"Murder or not, cut that beam! This is an order!"

The technician's hand reached for the switch. . . .

And the surge of power from the tap became an avalanche. An avalanche at the pole in the vertical plane of the planet's magnetic field where the winds of magnetism would not rise to blow it out.

One trillion watt-seconds of energy unleashed their fury on the polar cap in the first flash, as the negative charge of Atalama and the positive charge of its ionosphere surged to meet along the ionized pathway of the flare-augmented ionospheric tap beam.

But even as it discharged, the ionosphere was recharged from the solar furnace. The first flash became a mighty roar that poured an increased and now steady stream of more than 3×10^{20} watts of energy through the now-stabilized short circuit.

Kilocubit after square kilocubit of frozen wasteland boiled. Watt after watt of ever-increasing avalanche energy lit the polar cap with a glare that had never before been seen on Atalama.

Avalanche.

The passengers on the shuttle were unaware of their narrow escape. While the hellfire of unquenching avalanche burned at the pole they had just left, they calmly boarded the Vahsaba.

But there were those on board who knew of the disaster; who were watching the ever-increasing fury of the avalanche, driven wild by the unaccustomed force of the solar ultraviolet light being driven out in tremendous floods by the flare.

From this altitude, nineteen radii out, the avalanche was brighter than the sun itself, even on the apparently miniature replica of a world; the ring of compression advancing across the ice field was clear, but also miniature. A shock wave, racing at the speed of sound, it seemed merely to expand like a small smoke ring across the polar wastes. But it did not stop. It reached the edge of the ice and swept on down through the northerly latitudes, toppling great cities; and on down over the coastland. And yet the avalanche increased.

Its awesome fury was now sending fingered rivers of fire down through the continental faults, seeming to divide the continent itself into segments traced by a fiery knife.

Rahn spoke to his communications officer. "Contact the Aetalos, if you can. Let them know that we will stand by for whatever aid we can render."

But there was no contact. The roar of electrical energy was beyond the power of electronic apparatus to penetrate.

Forming in the great ring of shock wave, billowing clouds of steam from the polar cap were already obscuring the details of the fiery rivers that seemed to split the continent. But the rivers themselves were growing in length, reaching ever southward toward the mighty ocean.

The men in the Vahsaba were helpless. They could only sit and watch the destruction of their world.

Seven days they watched; the globe beneath them was now an unrecognizable shambles glowing with its own eerie light that centered the continuing finger of brilliant discharge at the pole.

Yet it depended on what timetable was accepted, the number of days. For now the planet no longer had the slow, majestic rotation that had once seemed as stable as eternity itself. Now it whipped about on its axis like a thing tortured, taking a mere one-fourth of its former time for a revolution of day and night.

Life was gone from the planet—of that Rahn was sure. Nothing, he told himself, could have survived the destruction they had witnessed. Just the radiation level that they could measure with the instruments aboard precluded the thought that anything could still live.

Yet he could not bring himself to give the command to take off that he knew he must give.

The theoreticians aboard predicted a final explosion of the planet itself, though not for some time yet.

"Consider it," Dade had explained the reasoning. "Consider the planet as a parallel field motor. The short circuit is robbing power not only from the ionosphere, but from the trapped charged particles in the radiation belts beyond the atmosphere.

"And in doing so, they are changing the magnetic field of the planet. It is as though you had decreased the magnetic field on an electric motor while maintaining power to the armature. The rotation will inevitably increase until the armature explodes. I advocate that we leave immediately, or be caught in the explosion!"

"You expect, then, this avalanche effect to

create that explosion?" Rahn asked carefully.

"Only indirectly. The explosion—which is now inevitable," Dade said fiercely, "will come about purely through centrifugal force, caused by the increase of rotation overcoming the gravitic force that holds the planet together.

"At the present rate of increase of speed, I predict that the continent will be torn apart sometime tomorrow—on its eighth day of increased spin. And that the planet itself will be subjected to a disruptive force sufficient to tear it apart within twenty-four days. It will explode, Rahn! And if you do not order the Vahsaba to leave now, you will be murdering the last remnants of our race!"

Rahn felt anger surging through the hopelessness that had come over them all. He spoke in a low, harsh monotone.

"Very well, Dade. I have heard you out. Now get off the bridge."

Yet when the man was gone, he knew he could not ignore the warning much longer. One more day, he told himself; one more day and night . . .

But even while he debated, Dade's first prediction was proven accurate. Below him, the continent of Ura began to tear—slowly, and then more rapidly as the hours passed, the continent was ripped asunder—ripped and torn, though the action could be seen only in bits and pieces through the tremendous storms that raged across its surface.

There was no longer any question. Rahn ordered the big motors warmed for the start of flight, and while they warmed, he watched. It would be a matter of hours before the Vahsaba was sufficiently powered, and he hoped he had not waited too long.

In those few hours, the precise gyroscope that was the planet unbalanced. A distinct precession appeared in the polar location . . .

Rahn checked his dials. The Vahsaba could not move—not yet—not for another two hours.

Below him the rent fragments of the continent were thrown violently across the surface of the planet; and then, with a mighty heave, the planet itself turned and tilted majestically, rotated nearly 45° . . .

And the avalanche, now in a latitude where the planet's magnetic force could have effect, went out—as suddenly and as completely as it had started.

The avalanche was ended, but Atalama was destroyed. Her land mass in huge blocks torn one from the other. Mountains where there had been plains. Churning seas beating savagely against the wounds of the land.

The two hours clocked past, and the big atomic motors that powered the Vahsaba roared into true life. Rahn made no motion to stay the ship, though Atalama's crisis was past, and the planet subsiding into a wounded quiet.

There was no other course than to take off, to find a new home for man. The planet was quiet, but the radiation raging in Atalama's atmosphere would not abate for centuries.

But men would return to their planet, Rahn told himself through clenched teeth.

The Vahsaba would return.

7

The engineer stared at the intense archaeologist. This was not a man telling a story, this was a man recounting a nightmare.

The desert stars pierced the night sky with a brilliance that the dry air did little to dim. Vaguely the engineer realized that he was shivering in the cold of the desert night.

"Who are you?" he asked. "And why have you told me this?"

"No," said the archaeologist in a deeply weary voice. "No. I am who you think I am." Then he stood suddenly and looked down at the seated engineer, and his voice became fierce.

"I'm telling you this," he said, "because they're back. Because they're using the same technology that has been used on this planet for our 'good' three times since the flood. They built Cheops in 3000 B.C., and blew up Sodom and Gomorrah over a misunderstanding in 2200 B.C. They nearly threw this planet into the sun when they blew up the fifth planet — Typhon — with their engineering in 1450 B.C. And they nearly blew it out again when their grid system backfired in 776 B.C.

"Not the Old Ones," he added in a softer tone, still fierce. "Not the ones who took a couple of thousand years of their new long lives to grow mature on a quiet planet with room to think and a job to do. But the New Ones; the ones who came back and took the long-grown know-how of the Old Ones and gadgetried it with their go-go ideas, and brought 'prosperity' — and havoc.

"They're back. And I can describe for you how their most recent — since about 2500 B.C. — technology works. And you've got to figure out how to build its duplicate. Their technology hasn't changed since they inherited it from the Old Ones in 2500 B.C., so we know they aren't growing; they haven't changed. And they may be ethical now and they may be high-minded; I don't know. Some of them were then, some weren't — but they're not growing, or their technology would have grown. And we're their 'run away and play now' children.

"If we want any say-so at all in what happens next, we have to grow up and match them now.

Right away. Yesterday, preferably.

"That's why I'm telling you."

The engineer stared long and hard out into the desert night. Finally he answered.

"It's a good thing," he said softly, "that I don't believe you. Because if I did . . ." He paused and took a deep breath. "If I did, I'd have to try to do what you ask."

The archaeologist slumped down onto his seat. "Will you hear the rest?" he asked.

"Oh, I'll hear the rest," the engineer answered. "If you wanted to stop, I'd have to try to persuade you to keep going. I've got a couple of sweaters" he added. "It's getting cold."

He pulled himself to his feet and went to a cardboard carton beside the small refrigerator, from which he pulled two sweaters — old army pullovers that had seen a bit of wear. He tossed one to the archaeologist, shrugged into the other. Then he grinned happily.

"By 'they're back' I suppose you mean the flying saucers?"

The archaeologist nodded. "The landing craft of the Vahs, and the 'viewer' transposers. There is no indication that the big transposers are in use yet."

"I'm glad you brought those in," said the engineer, his voice gay now. "You had me going for a minute. I was beginning to believe you. Now I can get my sense back and listen to the rest of the story. You haven't even gotten to the solar tap insulators — the pyramids — yet. How do you jump so fast to the — transposer?"

"Just one big pyramid in each area was a tap.

The Cheops in Egypt. The others are copies."

"No." The engineer's voice was stubborn. "If you're going to use those pyramids as proofs, be consistent. If you were right, the other pyramids would not be 'just copies' but very necessary to the system itself. You'd have one major laser-base and control system in a major insulator; and a series of lesser bases with satellite systems of laser beams. A single laser won't work. A single laser might ionize, if it were powerful enough, say, one hundred meters of path length near its focal point. A group of lasers packed together with slightly different focal points could ionize a nearly straight path — say, a thousand meters. But you wouldn't want a continuous ionized path from the ionosphere to ground in one fell swoop, anyhow. If you did that, you'd get much too big a splat of energy to be able to handle with any reasonable technology.

"So, say you take fifteen pyramids, just as a guess, and set them up in a pattern. Not all of them are very large, of course, and they serve two purposes. The lasers are mounted on them so that they have just the proper angle to form a step-ladder path from the ionosphere to ground. Firing them in sequence, you get the same sort of step-ladder reaction that you get from lightning bolts that zig and zag this way and that across the sky before finding a completely ionized path.

"I've no idea what the optimum zig zag path would be, but it probably wouldn't be exactly geometrical in terms of the location of the smaller pyramids. Anyhow, as I said, those lesser pyramids serve a second function. If you do get an *avalanche, there'll be one hell of an explosion over the main pyramid, and the shock wave from it will go racing across the plain on which your installation is located. So the second function of the smaller pyramids is to protect your multiple installation of secondary lasers. They will be mounted on the far side, away from the center of the explosion, and the pyramids will act as blockhouses."*

The archaeologist looked thoughtful. "So they all had their lapis lazuli. Their polished lasers. Not just the big ones." He smiled. "Thanks," he said. "You may be a scoffer, but you've just cleared up a mighty important point for me."

"But how do you jump from solar taps to transposers?"

The archaeologist looked at his host quizzically. "You developed the solar tap," he said. "You recognized the mechanics of the electromagnetic forces controlling the rotation of this planet, and you worked out the facts behind that pattern, and you devised a means for tapping into that powerful potential. You worked out that pattern in spite of the fact that traditional physics refuted you. Once the Van Allen belts were discovered, it became obvious to you how the planet is powered. So you could look behind the 'myths' of traditional physics and see how to tap that power.

"Yet when you read, almost daily, these days, of the factual use of transposers and landing craft here on this planet, you find it nonsense? Never mind," he added as the engineer started to interrupt, "there's more, and most of it I think you will

be able to recognize as well within our own technology, once we're using the tap. The planetary engineering job that was done to create the flood, for instance. You'll recognize that you could do the same job with the tap. The . . ."

"The flood?" The engineer smiled. "I gather you know how they did it?"

"I haven't described a thing that isn't possible to our own technology, that isn't in our own near future," the archaeologist stated almost fiercely. "And I don't think anything that's beyond us now has occurred in the last eighty-six hundred years."

The engineer leaned back, his pipe going nicely now, his interest real, his skepticism unalloyed. "I'm still listening," he said. "The flood?"

"Soon. When the Vaheva came back about 4400 B.C., she went into orbit, and searched the radio bands for a signal. Finally she caught the radio beam that Lord David had kept going. . . ."

David Lyon was busy at a small bench, checking through a standard chemical analysis, paying no attention at all to the occasional snap, hiss, or sputter of electrical energy faithfully reproduced by the webwork of gold and ceramics that was the electronic equipment he had set up so long ago to operate as a standby code beacon and receiver.

Aside from occasional inspection, it had required little of his time over the past centuries, and it was some minutes before he realized that the signals it was now emitting were not the random electronic noises of nature.

Faithfully the pendulum switch ticked over

and the device emitted a measured pulse of radio-frequency energy unheard on its own speaker, but radiating into space as an obvious man-made signal. Then, with the pendulum swing, the receiving function listened, the tiny gold-leaf speaker replicated the electronic signals that impinged upon it.

David's head came up. Signals. Not noise.

He listened with a feeling of unreality and a deep surge of—grief?

It's over, he thought.

Grief? he asked himself. Grief? It should be pleasure. The race of man exists outside of myself. It still exists. The time-space equations must have worked.

But the grief persisted, deep and full and very real, and he held from the switch and the key that he had kept in readiness. For how many years? For how many centuries?

I can hold my hand and they will go away, he thought . . . and the thought brought a rush of action that took his hand out to switch off the pendulum; and then to the key; and he began spelling out, in the old pulse code, the letters that he'd planned to use if this time ever came.

"This is Atalama. Who . . ."

Behind him there was a splatter of tiny hoof-clicks on the plastic floor, and the faun's hard little head bumped his arm abruptly from the key, its soft nose damply investigating the spot where his fingers had been. The instrument buzzed sharply, and the tiny animal sprang back, ears pointed, eyes bright with alarm.

David laughed and patted the rough velvet over

the bony cranium absently, then turned to the transmitter again. But the operator on the far end had recognized that the machine pattern had been replaced by a live transmission and had not waited, was already breaking in with a jittering, high-speed code—dots and dashes much too fast for the unskilled to read. David missed it completely.

Carefully he spelled out, "Slower, please. This is Atalama. Who calls?"

But the faun, its distrust of the buzz allayed by the assurance with which its master called forth the noises, was inquisitively bumping his arm again, ineffectively at first, then harder. Firmly, David took a grip on the slender neck and led the animal through to the garden area of the ship, closing the port behind him.

He returned quickly in time to hear, pulsed slowly now, as slowly as his own transmission had been, ". . . Vaheva, returning to Atalama. Where are you? We had given up hope that intelligent life was left."

David paused, then began the detailed pinpointing of his location. He couldn't use the grid system that had been in effect before, but he'd planned a system. "My area," he transmitted carefully, "is approximately twenty-eight degrees north of the equator. And I am in sunlight now, approximately . . ." he looked through an open port to the shadow dial on the foredeck, ". . . ten degrees past high noon. That, with the beacon signal, should give you sufficient information to find a large inland lake. The Juheda is in that lake, near the confluence of three rivers. We will leave off communication until you arrive since this is slow. Welcome home," he added. Then he paused a moment before he spelled out, "David Lyon, Lord of molecular biology, University of Créta," and released the key.

It was almost ten minutes before the instrument chattered again. "We plan to make planetfall about noon twenty-four hours from now," it spelled out, still slowly. "It will be good to see you, Lord Lyon." And the message was signed, "Jeris Gavarel, commanding Veheva, and all the crew."

David stood up from the small instrument that had quietly been sending its signals outwards over the centuries, and walked restlessly to the big easy chair on the far side of the laboratory that centered his activities these days. But his body refused to relax. He stood again and began pacing.

The race of man. It had returned in the persons of the crew of the Vaheva. Which meant that other ships, too, might return.

But what of my people? he thought. *What of the hu-man race? There will not, now, be the chance for them to demonstrate that a different evolutionary sequence can take a better form . . . or a worse.*

There's been no chance since the beginning, he told himself severely. *The radiation will be a hazard for another 10,000 years, and no race can survive that. The ability to become immune to the radiation has not shown up. The mutations have been too extensive.*

Even in Enoch and Noah's lines. Even there . . . though there'd been for a while a hope of immunity.

But why grief? he asked himself. The race of man has survived; the crew of the Vaheva will be sufficient to re-create the race again . . .

But the grief was there. Grief for his people, he thought; grief for the hu-man, who had not yet grown up; who would now never grow up, because they would be overrun; displaced before they had a chance to finish the fast re-evolution; before they show that with a new chance, the race could . . . might . . . would, possibly, produce something more mature.

The small craft made planetfall in the bay less than a kilocubit away, and was taxiing over easily. The first one to step from the lock was Captain Gavarel; immediately behind were Zad Shara and Memph Luce.

He watched them emerge and strap on their light heli-jets for the trip across to the Juheda with growing amazement.

The eye forgets, he thought. *How different they were—are—from my people.*

They came aboard, and he welcomed them gladly and with a pleasure that grew more intense in their company. Zad's lithe easiness; Jeris Gavarel's nearly ponderous humor, out of place in the compact, medium-sized body; Memph Luce, as handsome of dark face and flashing eye as before. Such familiar strangers, he thought, striving to force himself back into the old communication patterns.

The grief was gone now. He had let it play itself out during the hours before they were to arrive. Now he could fully allow himself the pleasure of their company.

Yet—they seemed so young. Not in their faces or bodies, but in their attitudes. He found himself deeply amused. Twenty-two hundred years makes a difference in the attitudes of living, he decided wryly.

He was trying to explain what had happened without taking forever to do it. He found himself picking and choosing between words, between facets of the problems that he'd faced, between nuances and direct threads.

At his feet the faun lay, its slender legs delicately curved for relaxation or the quick spring of flight; its soft nose sniffing the new odors with delight.

"We were nine that survived the seven days. Do you know," he interrupted himself with sudden pleasure, "that since you landed you have told me more of what happened than I had learned in twenty-two hundred years? Of course, we surmised and extrapolated but we were underseas, which is what saved us during the whole thing. We had to surmise the rest, for we are confined to a small part of the surface. We knew the day had changed length, and that the planet had rolled—we could tell that from the stars." He paused, and the pause lengthened.

Zad was watching him intently from an easy chair, shadowed in the corner. Now she spoke softly. "You were nine left . . ."

"Yes," he said. "Nine. Not for long, though. The

others left in the first few decades. All but Bon. Bon Hindra. The other Atalamans—they must explore. They must . . . do anything except that which had to be done."

He took a deep breath. There was really no use trying to tell them—the years, the hopes, the fears, the . . . "We had regeneration. Perfecting that took only a few more years. I had been wrong about the need for a closed ecology. Regeneration is a memory-tap function. Chemical assists are helpful, especially the ones I worked out for animals, where they develop a shell and regenerate, like Faunus here. But in the main, it's a problem of redefining the acquired information at the level of cellular function; memory-tap handling of electronic/biochemical patterns . . ."

He paused a moment. Then: "But . . . we thought we were the last of the race of man, you know. We were pretty sure we were the last on the planet. Even if some had survived, the radiation was so intense. We were sure we were the last," he ended quietly.

"Tell us about your people. They're so lovely and light. They're so delicate—like your faun." It was Zad's voice again. David was glad the others were letting her do the speaking. Her voice was a chord of music to an ear too long denied.

"The people of the Juheda." he smiled. "It took nearly six hundred years before we got Adam, our first hu-man." He nudged the faun gently with his toe and was rewarded with a tiny whinny. "This one's ancestors were a great help in that work. We tried all sorts of techniques for getting a viable species from cells of males, bypassing what we

didn't have—a capable female. After the prelimi-
nary work we developed an entirely new strain
from the faun—a much larger animal, still affec-
tionate toward man, but large enough to be a help,
too.

"Then we had the techniques and could
develop the hu-man from our own cells as we had
developed the hu-faun from faun cells."

David caught a questioning look on Zad's face,
and shook his head. "This one," he indicated the
faun again, " . . . no. He's neither an original
descendant or the hu-faun I was speaking of. He's
been with me for more than a thousand years, the
only successful animal experiment in regeneration."

His voice stopped, and there was silence. *But if I
make it sound this way,* he thought, *the whole
thing becomes portentous and melodramatic.
These are children yet, to whom I speak. How
shall I tell them of the wonder of life reborn? Of
the true magnificence of those years spent in
search of a result –- and the result achieved? Of
the race of man with a new chance — a future?*

"Then," he said, "we had a bit more know-how,
but not much. But we had to have a woman. This
was the new race, the hu-man race. How we
worked!" His voice boomed back at him through
the room, and he realized the surge of feeling was
too powerful. He quieted a moment, then went on.
"At last we decided to take cells from our male's
body and use those.

"There was, you see, an additional problem to
that of merely producing a woman. And this you
must understand. The male was a throwback in

some ways—not so much to an earlier evolutionary form as to an emptier mind than that with which the normal man-child is born; and a much less rapidly maturing body. It was as though the mind had been wiped clear of all the idiocies and the stupidities and the cantankerous bits and pieces than mankind has built into himself.

"The full convoluted cerebrum was present; of that we were sure. But it was a clean slate, unprogrammed, or a much more nearly clean slate, on which the evolution of man was to be rewritten. That evolution would be rapid in terms of normal evolution, because the physical evolutionary product was intact; it was a matter of the reprogramming of the intact cerebrum. The development of millennia could be compacted into a few centuries.

"But I felt . . . we felt . . . that something much better might develop, since mankind seemed to have been given a second chance—a clean, fresh chance, to develop as a sentient, self-aware animal. And this chance we must not lose.

"I hoped—and we succeeded—in getting a woman from the patterns inherent in the cell structure of the male."

He stopped again, but there was no sound in the big lounge room of the Juheda. He looked from one to the other of them—Jeris Gavarel, listening with a quiet that made his body seem immobile, even its breathing hushed. Memph Luce leaning forward, his handsome face intent, his eyes brilliant with interest. And Zad, fingers clutched in her lap, curled like a kitten into her chair, her eyes never leaving him.

"Our intent," David continued softly into the stillness, "was to keep them regenerative until they matured as sentient beings. Regeneration and reproduction are not mutually exclusive properties, you know—of course you don't know. But the reproductive function interferes with the emotional stability necessary to learn, to develop, the regenerative ability.

"Then, too, it was necessary, I thought, for them to learn and evolve considerably more than normal between generations so as to decrease the overall evolutionary period. The more experience an individual passes on to his children, the more evolved those children become—each generation makes real progress, rather than replaying the same old record, adds something vital to the evolutionary trend.

"So we hoped to keep them regenerative and to work with them through centuries until we found what the cerebral evolutionary result would be.

"Anyhow, we could obviously not keep a reproductive group of people aboard the Juheda and under ideal laboratory conditions. But they didn't wait for us to decide when the change should take place.

"I was shocked when I finally noticed the girl was pregnant." Lord David smiled. "I teased her about swallowing an apple seed, but of course we had to put them ashore."

Then he chuckled to himself. "Such lovely children—and such children! I asked Eve how she had known how to make love. She said that Adam's little snake had told her." He chuckled again. "I don't doubt it," he said. "Adam was a right lusty young male. I asked him how he'd known, and he said that his snake had taught Eve, and Eve had taught him. He seemed to feel no responsibility at all for his 'snake.' " David relaxed and a distant look came into his eyes.

"Eve gave us quite a scare about then. All of her curiosities were coming into full flood at the same time, and she was an inquisitive little bit—as inquisitive and as lovely as Faunus, here. She got hold of one of the wires of what they called my 'tree of light', and knocked herself out. Bon and I were frantic, but it was just a small electrical shock, and I don't think did much harm. But she never touched the tree of light again.

"However, she was pregnant, and it was time for them to fly the nest. It was time for separation. We showed them films—they called our projector the 'tree of knowledge.' We showed them training films on childbirth and farming and animal husbandry. I think it was a mistake. I think those films were too far beyond their understanding, and that they frightened them rather than teaching them. But we were trying to give them all the knowledges we could. We couldn't make tools for them, or farm for them, or take care of their animals. That would have been against the pattern. We had to let them grow up their own way. But we could show them how. I think the things we showed them personally, the how-to's that we demonstrated ourselves, were effective. But the films just scared them.

"Then we put them in a safe place. They didn't know we guarded or helped them; they had to think they were completely on their own. But of course we did."

He looked at their serious faces. Were they understanding the problem—the tremendous opportunity—that had been given into the hands of those aboard the Juheda? A new chance for man to develop, to evolve, as an ethical creature, clean, without the quarrelsome, built-in ego blocks that had come so near to destroying the race of man so frequently? To evolve with respect for his body as a healthy, functioning organism; and for his mind as an intelligence with a potential much greater than had ever been achieved? As an intelligence with knowledge as its conscious goal? A clean slate—a rebirth at an evolutionary point where the cerebrum was intact, but not—discolored.

They must understand! But Bon hadn't—apparently couldn't understand; and if they didn't grasp the factor intuitively, then he, David knew—knew by the bitterest of experience—that it would not be grasped.

"When they became reproductive, it became a question of the people evolving as versus those who would be needed to guide that evolution. There had to be separation—a minimum of contact, a minimum of influence or rules or guidance of any sort.

"So we built a guarded area for them ashore, at the confluence of the three rivers. And we put them ashore. We knew the radiation would be a mutation hazard. It was one to which we thought they might—they still might—develop an immunity. But there was no other chance. So we

created for them domestic animals as we created
the babustin and the cannus for you, we picked a
spot where the mutated animal life forms were
scarce, and we gave them protection. And we put
them ashore."

Jeris Gavarel spoke then; softly, as though not
wanting to interrupt David's train of thought. "We
saw their fields and their grazing animals as we
came down. They've reproduced, I gather, quite
successfully. There must have been several
thousand."

"Yes. Several thousand of the ones here. I have
the genealogies." David paused then. "The ones
here in the guarded area are not all," he said.

"The first disruption of the Juheda came as the
first two male children matured. One of the two
turned out to have retained the murderous instincts that I had hoped were now gone from the
race. He killed his brother. Over a preference he
thought I had shown for his brother!" He smiled
grimly, then went on.

"You could hardly be expected to understand
the depths of the emotions that swept the Juheda
then, and divided us. Think. We'd lived and
worked together then for several centuries. We'd
created together. And now we were torn asunder.
For if man were to re-evolve as an ethical
animal—and the evolution, this time, should not
take more than a few thousand years—then this . . .
throw-forward? Yes. I think you could call it a
throw-forward, rather than a throwback—to the
murderous instincts with which man had survived before—must not be allowed to breed into
the race. Yet Bon—you remember him, Zad? He

felt as strongly that this was the survival instinct at work, and that if there were to be a race of man again, it must be bred into the race.

"It was an open-and-shut choice. There could be no compromise on a choice like that. The experiment proceeded one way or the other, and no starships had returned. They should have returned from the shorter voyages within decades after the avalanche, and either they did not return or they did not find us. But because they had not returned, we were convinced that we were the last remaining members of our race, custodians of its survival, with the responsibility for seeing that that survival proceeded in the best interests of the race. So you can see, there could be no compromise.

"It was not a question that we decided hastily, and we were divided. Finally, Bon took the one carapet that we had. He took the murderous male and two females, and they left. He planned to go into the mountains far to the east, where we felt the radiation might be less intense. He had atomic batteries and could have gone great distances. We had hoped to keep in touch by radio, but we have never made radio contact, and I can only assume that he met with an accident."

"You've been alone? For hundreds of years?" It was Memph who spoke now, slowly, his deep attachment for the biologist evident in his tone.

"More than fifteen hundred years. Yes. But not quite alone all the time. Twice I have taken one of my people aboard to live with me, to train, to teach. They must school themselves in the sciences of the lordorate as rapidly as possible. I have taught them that when they grow up, as soon as they can understand, that they will come into the knowledge of the Lord. That it is theirs. That I am only their father, guarding that knowledge for them which is their heritage. That they must grow into it, must school themselves until they can understand it.

"And when I have had one of them with me, it has been not only for my own solace, to have a living sentient being here, but in order that the fact of the knowledge which is theirs may have reality to them; that they can know it as a fact, that it is here, that it will not be lost. That they shall have physical contact with the appurtenances of knowledge through members of their tribes.

"Of course, I can't take one of them in until he has raised many children; for I must select of the best, and those genes and that gentleness must not be lost to the race. Their normal life span is as many centuries as mankind's is decades, however, to that it's a small problem."

"Their normal life span is what?" Jeris Gavarel asked.

David looked up. Of all the account that he had given them, this one thing seemed to have gotten a startle-reaction. *Children,* he thought. *These, too, are children.*

"Oh, yes," he said casually. "They do not mature physically—do not enter puberty—in less than one hundred years. And normally they live six to eight hundred years beyond that. I have the records here," he said.

8

The engineer stood up abruptly. "That's a pretty strong story you're telling," he said fiercely.

The archaeologist nodded. "I find that truth is stronger than fiction," he said quietly. "I find truth far harder to swallow than — than the pap we have been fed across the various credibility gaps."

Then, abruptly fierce himself, he added, "But the biologist refused to feed pap across the credibility gap. The pap comes later. He never — not once — told his people other than that he was their guardian, their father. He told them that health and knowledge — a sound mind in a sound body — were the ideal; and that the knowledge of the Lord — the knowledge of the civilization and its universities that had been before — was theirs by right. That it was theirs just as fast as they could comprehend and absorb it.

"He never, by thought or deed or implication, set himself up as a god. That was the Cha-Ra — the transposer people. That began around 2300 — and when he came back and found that it had happened, he threw the transposer people back to their planets and cut the connection; and he did his level best to wipe out the effects of what they had done — physical and mental.

"That's when he selected the tribe of Abraham and tried to put it back on the evolutionary track again; clean it up, physically and morally. He'd thrown the Cha-Ra off the planet, and he tried to wipe out the damage they'd done. He couldn't handle what had become nearly a planetful of people, but he could get one tribe back.

"Then he had to leave again because he had Enoch and his family growing up on another planet.

He paused, then ended abruptly. "Yes. It's a pretty strong story. And it took intelligence and gentleness and love . . . and a lot of other qualities . . . to . . ." His voice ran down and he sat silent for a long time.

"You get all this out of the Bible?" the engineer asked finally.

The archaeologist's sudden shout of laughter startled him. "Ye gods and little fishes, no! This is one planet, with one coherent, readable geological and archaeological record. It is one people— the human race, with admixtures that have been thrown in from time to time, mostly violently. The

dates I've used may be inexact—you should read
them as plus or minus a couple of centuries—but
the pattern of dates, the sequence of events, shows
everywhere, from Egypt to the Andes, from India
to England, from China through Samoa and
Hawaii, North America and Africa. Aesland. It's a
consistent, graphable sequence, and each sub-
division of the human race shows it.

"For instance, the Sumerians weren't histo-
rians, as the Hebrews were, but S. N. Kramer, one
of the foremost of our Sumeriologists, thinks they
wrote their tens of thousands of clay tablets before
the Hebrews wrote down the Old Testament. I
think Kramer's wrong; original records were simply written on destructible material, though
sketchily kept from 4400 to 2200 B.C., and have
been lost; but that's a moot point. Certainly the
Sumerian tablets go back to almost 3000 B.C., and
show the same pattern until the race was wiped
out when Typhon — the fifth planet of our system,
where the asteroid belt is now — when Typhon
blew in 1450 B.C.

"At any rate, the Sumerian records show Lord
David as 'An,' probably pronounced 'Aeion,'—
the first one. And they list the immortals — the
'seven originals and fifty who came later' — as
Anunnaki — the 'Aitons of An'? In Greece, Lord
David is 'Ur-Aenos,' born from the wind blown
egg of the sea of chaos in the beginning. Zad,
Memph, Pat Tos and Jack Kronus and the other
three who stayed behind when the Vaheva left
after the flood, are the Taetons. The fifty who
stayed behind from the next ships are the lesser
Taetons.

"In Egypt (or 'Aegypt') the Aetum, or Amon was
the first one, while the seven (or eight — there is
some question) who stayed from the Vaheva were
the Eniad, or Aeniad. Then came the transposer
people and you get the Cha-Ra and the Pha-rae.
By 2200 you have at least four ships back, and at
least two sets of transposer people — people who
have come in the big ships, then gone back to their
planets to build transposer 'gates' and come
through. You have the Aryans, and the Minoans
and the Vahsaba'alem and the Vahsatanaian . . .

"Or take the word for solar taps. 'Cheops,' in
Egypt; or maybe 'Shi-ops' is a closer pronuncia-
tion. And the other sites that provided multiphase
control: the one in Cambodia at Angkor Wat; and
on the Yucatán peninsula, Teotihuacan, which I
will bet was originally pronounced 'Shi-
opihuacan' and may be today. There's one in
South America, too. In India the name comes
down as 'Shi-Vah'; and probably China took its
name from the same source — Chi-nah. In Greece,
the taps were known as the Cyclops, which was
most likely originally 'Shi-ops.' In Sumerian, the
tap is the 'Enlil', or 'Aenlil' — the eye of the
Anunnaki. On your dollar bill, it's just a pyramid
with an eye.

"Or the sites of the various transposers? I can
tell you where most of them were, and it's not
guesswork. Exact spots. They're in every mythology, too — the monsters with the hundred hands
and fifty heads, that spit fire and brimstone three
times. They were also the dark entrances to the
'nether worlds,' as 'far below earth as is earth
below heaven.' The nether world that is some-

times to the north and bitter cold; and sometimes
to the south and is hell-hot; and that during the
time of the transposer people was guarded by —
well, Enki, in Sumerian, to protect the 'divine
laws' — the electricity of Enlil, the Cheops, from
the original immortals who didn't at all like what
the transposer people were doing.

"If you want evidence, I can give you an Ency-
clopaedia Britannica of it. It's there. Geologic,
historic, mythologic, semantic, archaeologic —
factual. But . . . you're determined this is just a
story, remember?" And he laughed again.

"Hmmph. A melting pot of civilized peoples
and technological barbarians existing as a
superstructure over a primitive culture — even a
primitive people would have noticed what was
going on, and questioned it."

"But — you don't understand! Neolithic. The
hu-man race didn't begin to reach the primitive
level until about 60 A.D. The early primitive
level. Lord David started with — well, does your
dog question electricity? Human beings with no
patterns in the cerebrum! A full cerebral structure
— and none of the patterns of thought that had
built with it over the millennia to make a race
capable of technology. They were biologically
capable of holding the detail you handle today,
but with none of the cerebral patterns of thought
written in! Blank. Survival abilities at an animal
level.

"Of course, given those factors inherent in the
problem, an exponential scale of development is
predictable; and you have what John Campbell
called the 'exploding genetic heritage' factor. A

tribe develops patterns of know-how. This makes it possible for them to dominate their neighbors, to conquer and spread. Their know-how genetic structure is diluted when they spread, now their neighbors have the gene patterns in diluted form, too, and begin to grow faster.

"But . . . in those early stages, I rather imagine that the high-psi animals brought in by the Wytches and probably used as monitors over the people had actually more cerebrally effective intelligence than the humans. They didn't have the cerebral capacity to acquire more; but what capacity they had had the written-in information intact.

"However, the people did notice. They worshiped and served the 'gods.' Only Abraham's tribe served as slaves and worshiped only the Lord — until somebody else took over the Lord's voice after a catastrophe, when they began obeying orders that came over the ark-radio-transmitter. The hu-mans acted as servants in the twenty thousand 'temples' of the city of Pagan, for instance. Those temples were merely the homes of the transposer peoples. The hu-mans mined for the 'gods' through the big transposer bases at Sodom and Gomorrah.

"Oh, they noticed. They just didn't understand."

"All right," said the engineer, surprised to find himself growing furious. "It's just a story. So I'm going to pick at it in an area where I have some know-how. That flood. The carbon 14 was a diffuse gas admixture of the carbon-dioxide content of the atmosphere. How does a flood get it out?"

"Oh," said the archaeologist, chuckling. "You diluted it and added carbon 12. Or rather, first you increased the carbon 12 dioxide ... It wasn't just a flood, of course. They had to take all the factors into consideration in their planning. . . ."

It began as a captain's conference, in the small quarters he used as an office.

Zad sat in a straight chair beside Memph, against the wall, watching the captain making notes at his desk as they talked; watching Lord David, sitting quietly in an easy chair in the corner; watching Ted Promo, the Vaheva's chief engineer, and his second, Pat Tos, in the formal chairs beside the captain's desk; while Jack Kronus sat on a corner of the desk, his lanky frame relaxed against the wall.

From the corner of her eye she watched, too, as one or two and then four or five crew members paused beside the open office door to listen, leaning against the door jamb and the far wall. The Vaheva, having planted its colony, had taken on an informality that—*that makes us a team,* she thought; an informality that was instinct of respect from top to bottom . . . and from bottom to top. *They obey their captain as a leader, not a master,* she thought; *they respect him as an able man . . . and his authority is unquestioned.*

The captain, his face away from the door, had not apparently noticed the growing audience, so that it caught Zad by surprise when he remarked dryly, still without looking towards the open doorway, "This is a matter for the entire personnel, most of which seems to be interested already." Permitting himself a small smile, he turned towards the door. "We will adjourn to the lounge," he said.

By the time the formal conference members reached the lounge, most of the crew was there already waiting. The absentees could be counted as those on duty roster. *The word spreads fast,* thought Zad, and grinned at the thought. *The grapevine is still the fastest means of communication.*

The captain seated himself on the edge of a big table that centered on the lounge, and gestured to Promo and Pat to take places beside him. David selected an easy chair at the corner of the table, and Zad and Memph found chairs nearby.

"The problem appears to be twofold," Jeris Gavarel stated formally, letting his eyes range over the gathering. Young, all of them. Able, again, all of them. *Well,* Zad told herself, *we've a test, here, of that ability.*

"First there's Lord David's people—a new race, with a fast evolutionary potential that may take them past the rest of us if given the opportunity. What we need to do is set up the opportunity for a race that may prove to be superior to us in the long run. Anybody object to that?" He paused a moment, but there was no answer except a muttered, "Chelt, no. If they can do better, let 'em," from somewhere nearby.

"Okay." The captain's voice sounded pleased. "The parameters of the problem are that the race doesn't have one evolutionary chance in ten thousand so long as they're up against the heavy carbon 14 radiation that the avalanche put out. That's one.

"The other parameter is this: The new race doesn't have one really evolutionary chance in ten thousand if we put a technological colony down beside 'em. They'd just grow up as subsidiary members of an already established civilization. I don't know what their true potential is, but Lord David thinks it's very superior. He's spent two dozen centuries getting them this far, and he ought to know. Now, given the parameters of the problem, what's to do about it?"

"Get rid of the radiation, and then get damn well out," came a deep voice from Zad's right.

Gavarel waited a few minutes, but that was the only suggestion, with a few scattered assents following.

"Very well," he said. "I take that as a consensus. That leaves us with only one major problem. Getting ourselves out of here is easy. How do we get rid of the radiation?"

Promo stirred, and the captain turned to his chief engineer.

"Well—I was thinking about it last night. First you'd have to put heavy concentrations of carbon 12 into the atmosphere. Until you got, in the carbon-dioxides themselves, a normal proportion between the 12s and the 14s. You always have some 14s, of course," he added.

"Then you'd have to wash out all the carbon dioxides you could—get the atmosphere back to the normal carbon-dioxide percentage. Once you'd gotten the proportions between the 12s and the 14s right, you have to get the total percentage in respect to the atmosphere back to normal. Then probably add some more carbon 12-dioxide for good measure. Not too much. That ought to do it."

Lord David was looking at the engineer with some awe. "You're talking about the entire planetary atmosphere?"

Ted Promo looked back at the biologist, pleasure on his face. "You were talking about the whole race of man when you thought you were 'surviving' them," he said. "Yes. I'm talking about the whole atmosphere of the planet. In one sense, though, you should remember that the carbon-dioxide content of the atmosphere is less than one percent of the atmosphere; and we need change it to not more than—say—five times its present amount. It helps to get some perspective to realize that by weight the whole atmosphere is less than one part per hundred thousand of the planet. There's enough carbon dioxide trapped in the rocks, as carbon dioxide, to replace the whole atmosphere several times over without even referring to the trapped fossil carbons such as coal.

"But it's going to be drastic, if we do it," he added solemnly. "I'm talking about volcanoes and floods. I'm talking about taking the atmosphere up to near-lethal before bringing it back down again to a livable level. You sure it's a good idea? I'm talking about floods—real floods. We'd have to melt the polar caps. That ought to get a water table rise of—say—two hundred feet. Nothing but mountains above the flood level. Of course your hu-men could go to the mountains, but there'd be real violent storms, and . . . then there would be the volcanoes. We'd have to— chelt, we'd have to activate a hundred or more to throw up enough carbon 12. They'd throw up everything and its brother besides, but the rest of the stuff would precipitate out. It normally does. But, raising the carbon 12 level would mean volcanoes erupting, and then erupting again.

"I'm talking about a clean-up job, David, that may be more lethal than your mutations."

"I think," David Lyon replied quietly into a room of such intent silence that his words fell like pebbles into an abyss, "I think that my people are doomed if the radiation continues to its own natural decay point. I've been graphing the increasing mutations, and they've nearly reached the exponential break. In another few hundred years, there would be no recognizable hu-man left. So that it becomes a question of extremes. Your planetary engineering would at least give some of them a chance."

He was silent then, and no one in the room interrupted the silence until he continued, "We on the Juheda were a very small group—but we survived the avalanche, which included the breakup of the continent and the creation of mountains. I doubt if you will match the fury of that event. And we survived in a ship. I could have my people build similar ships. Then, they have at least a chance. If they survive, they survive. They will have had a chance."

Zad felt a shiver run down her spine. *How—how old he is,* she thought. *But—how right.*

Promo slowly uncoiled his lean figure from the edge of the table, reached as though for a pen, then stuck his hands determinedly in the pockets of the ship's regulation coveralls that he wore. *He thinks better with pen and paper,* thought Zad.

"Well, look," he said. "The planet's an electric motor; its design is somewhat similar, actually, to the design of the Vaheva—or rather, that's backwards. We built the Vaheva on the planet's design, more or less. At any rate, it's a form of electric motor and electric generator, and it generates a lot more power than the Vaheva. So what we have to do is use the power of the planet itself to create the effect we want—volcanic action, floods, and torrents of rain. The minimum necessary effect—but it'll be a real doozy of a minimum.

"Now the electrons from the solar wind come in at the pole and take two directions—three, actually, but the third's a minor one. They split off through the ionosphere and out through the proton and electron belts held in the magnetic field. There's some seepage of atmospheric electricity at lower levels—that's the minor effect.

"But by far the largest proportion of the planet's electrical current is self-generated by dynamo action, and exists as a flow through the silicate layer above the core—just under the mantle—where there's the least resistance. It creates sufficient heat to keep the silicate layer molten and its conductivity high. That current represents a drag on the motor, a conversion of a large part of the motor's energy to heat. And, incidentally, creates the sustaining magnetic field that regulates the motor.

"Now, if we speed the rotation of the planet up about ten percent, we'll increase the flow of electrons from the solar wind across the ionosphere, and also increase the dynamo effect in the core. If we put sodium vapor into the ionosphere, we

cause additional current from the combination
photoelectric effect and the reduction of the ionization potential. At the same time, the sodium
vapor will act as a radiant energy absorber, taking
in and trapping a larger quantity of heat directly
from the sun, heating the atmosphere by
greenhouse effect, and, incidentally, making
some beautiful sunsets.

"The combination should melt the polar caps.
There's your floods. At least two hundred feet of
extra water. Then, the heat from the core and the
increase of the jet streams of air high in the atmosphere should cause torrential rains. The electric
pressure on the atmosphere should increase—I'd
think you might build up to as much as two at-
mospheres pressure; and this should increase the
'Shi' effect which builds storms into self-
sustaining hurricanes. You've got your volcanoes
going by now, which should contribute to the
greenhouse effect, and to the storms, as well as
adding their own little sideshow to the circus."

"What's the trigger on the volcanoes?" someone called out.

"Oscillating magnetic flux in the crust." That
would be Jack's quiet voice, Zad decided, but he
was off to the right, where she couldn't see him.

"How you gonna get that magnetic flux to oscil-
late?" another voice asked. "It's got to be a pretty
active oscillation."

Promo smiled briefly in Jack Kronus's direction,
and the youngster climbed to his feet. "Throw up
some copper wires. Tiny ones. Get a few bales of
them spread out and orbiting in the
ionosphere—you'll get your oscillations of flux,"

he said. Then he added, "Ever read about the time back on Atalama, when we were experimenting with rocket power before the Baron discovered the Sivas? They orbited a batch of copper wires—I think they meant to get radio reflection or something. Had the damnedest series of earthquakes from the oscillating flux effect, but they never did recognize what caused them. They didn't send up enough to get more than minor grumbles out of the volcanoes, though. We'll orbit, I'd think, about twice as many as were used then, and get some real sweet volcanic action. Inch-long, hair-fine, orbiting copper wires. Best things possible to stir up crustal action." He grinned at the group and sat down again.

Promo's voice took up again. "The whole pattern should build up to critical in a very short time—say a few months. Should take only one Siva, if we can find a salt bed somewhere. We can use the Siva to refine the sodium vapor and to throw it into the ionosphere when we get enough refined." He stopped as abruptly as he had started, and leaned against the edge of the table.

"How're we gonna stop it once we get it started?" a voice called. "That should work to start it. Now—how're we gonna turn it off and get the floods gone and the volcanoes quiet?"

"Chlorine." This time it was Pat Tos who spoke up, his freckled face bright with excitement, his blue eyes turned on Ted Promo with almost embarrassing admiration. "You've got to get the chlorine out of the salt to get pure sodium vapor. Just combine it with hydrogen—that'll even help the effect—and store it under as much pressure as you can get it in a dark place. Then—well, you could explode it with a light bulb when you were ready, and it would generate sufficient energy of explosion to take it on up to where the sodium vapor was. You couldn't operate a Siva from beneath a flood, so you'd have to have some method like that for getting your 'brakes' up to the proper spot. Once the chlorine got up there, it would combine with the sodium vapor and precipitate."

Promo nodded hugely. "Chlorine would do it," he said, "and it would combine the two operations into one. You take out the chlorine while you're refining the sodium, store the one, and toss up the other."

"How would the chlorine work?" asked David.

"Well . . ." Promo reached toward his pen again, then stopped himself. "First it would reduce the ionosphere ionization; it would tend to stop the electron flow. It would also combine with the sodium vapor to create sodium chloride, which would precipitate out of the atmosphere. The precipitation will take quite a while longer than the time it takes to get the stuff up there in the first place, but . . . well, the electrical action should stop rather quickly. We'll have to send the chlorine up a bit at a time, or the brakes would go on too hard."

"Just tank the chlorine, Pat says," called a voice. "You think we've got a metallurgical civilization here to build us tanks? Or that we could set up for that in—well, it would take decades."

Pat laughed. "Oh, we ought to be able to find a geological formation—say a gas field—that we can drill a tap hole into and pump the chlorine into under pressure. The gas—methane—would provide the required hydrogen. Should be some trap-domes in all these new mountains."

"Say." The voice was excited, from somewhere on her right, Zad decided. "Instead of using an open salt bed, why don't we look for a salt dome formation? Then we could put the chlorine back in where we extract the salt out, after we get the sodium out of it. We can put the Siva nearby, use it for the extraction and refining as well as for putting the sodium topside. And," the voice added, "we'd better refine about an extra twenty percent of chlorine to take care of possible seepage losses or combination losses during storage. We want to be sure we can stop this thing."

The voices came thick and fast then. As far as Zad could tell, the chlorine sent up after the washup would combine with the sodium vapor, precipitate out, lower the planet's "armature current," and cool it about ten percent below the present temperature. The polar caps would again begin to form and within a year or so the sea would be withdrawn; estimates ranged, but the consensus was that the waters would go about five percent below their present level and probably stay there. The crew seemed to agree that the withdrawal process might take up to ten years to complete—maybe more. And that the extra land exposed—about five percent—might well be a permanent exposure.

The group broke up, finally; excited, jubilant, happy. Technical details were being worked out as fast as they were being proposed. Nobody asked whether the crew of the Vaheva would be willing to remain to do the job. They'd have gotten a blank stare of incomprehension had they asked. Yet it would take at least two years—one to set it up, one to supervise the return to normal—and they'd be two years of hard work. That was inherent in the problem.

Zad smiled softly. *What a crew*, she thought. And what on Ura—she corrected herself—what on the five continents did they need with a mentor? *I'm just excess baggage*, she told herself severely.

Then she went to find Lord David. It took a while, but she finally located him in the crew cafeteria, withdrawn, at a corner table, watching the bustle of activity.

She seated herself opposite him quietly, returned his smile, then asked, "What about your people, David? We could bring at least two thousand of them aboard the Vaheva."

He smiled. "Better than that," he said. "This is a new race, Zad. They should be seeded in more than one spot. I think Enoch and his family and I will hitch a ride aboard the Vaheva to a new planet, if Captain Gavarel will find us one. Enoch has been my companion for some years, and his family is in relatively good condition. About a thousand of them, I think."

"And we'll help build boats for the others," Zad said happily.

"No." He said it positively, and Zad looked at him in surprise. "That's a decision I had to make a long time ago. It is against the nature of the problem. They must survive of themselves. They must do their own learning."

She continued to look at him, wonderingly, and he frowned a bit before going on. "When I put them in the guarded area," he said, "I selected a protected place, but they had to guard themselves. I showed them how to build fire, but they had to build the fires. I showed them how to fire clay, but they fashioned their own utensils. I showed them how to chip stone, but they made their own implements.

"No," he said. "I will tell them of the coming floods. I will tell them what to build and how to build. I will caution them to save the animals, too—the domestic animals and what they can of the wild ones. And plants and life-forms of all sorts. But they must do the job themselves; and if they will not do it, then we shall see whether they can take to the mountaintops and survive when the times comes.

"I will," he said, " . . . if they build boats, I will put in remote-controlled motors—preferably without their knowing it. I will give them a hand. That is a father's prerogative. But I will not—nor will I let any of you—do it for them. Zad, you see that, don't you? You see that they must do that of themselves?"

She nodded slowly. *What a people they will be,* she thought. With this man for mentor, and a clean slate from which to start—what a people must develop!

9

"Enoch?" asked the engineer.

"Enoch. Remember 'And Enoch walked with the Lord after he begat Methuselah three hundred years, and begat sons and daughters. And all the days of Enoch were three hundred sixty and five years. And Enoch walked with the Lord, and he was not; for the Lord took him . . . '"

The engineer shivered. "You make it sound so real," he said, unhappily. "But of course if you fit your story to the data available . . ."

"I haven't tried to 'fit a story,' " said the archaeologist softly. "I started in 1936 trying to see what the stories said, when I realized that nobody had made them up; that they were, in fact, like a small child trying to explain how Momma got him a baby sister. I've tried to look at the archaeological evidence, and the geological evidence and the historic evidence, and listen to the myths and the legends . . . and hear what they had to say. Find the pattern. You gave me the missing factor when you published the theory of the solar tap.

"It's a complex pattern," he said. "But when you see the pattern, the pieces fall into place. All the pieces, if you've seen the right pattern."

"All right, then. I'll pick at your pattern again." The engineer spoke grimly. "These 'Vahnire' returning. So many of them? All immortals? Doesn't make sense. Some of them would still be here."

"Not all immortals. By no means, all immortals. Lord David, some of the crew of the Vaheva, and the seven who stayed after the flood when the Vaheva left. Perhaps — though I'm not convinced–the fifty who remained from the Vahs that arrived after the flood and who stayed behind while their ships went back to put transposer units on their home planets.

"Immortality, regeneration—takes ability and consistent work and concentration. How many people do you know who can concentrate? Really concentrate? No. Immortality is the hallmark of the most able because it cannot be achieved by the unable."

"All right. But so many mortals here that were far enough outside the normal pattern to be worshiped as gods? And so little evidence?"

"But there is evidence!" The archaeologist's voice was exasperated. "Earth was a colonial planet to the 'far ones.' In a colonial area you expect to find fine, technologically serviced homes adjacent to native hovels. And you find them. Palaces. Temples. Count the number of really big, magnificent, necessarily technologically-serviced palaces and temples that predate — well, take 2200 B.C. There are literally thousands of them. Mostly set up with a religious order — the priests as house-servants, the people as the laborers. In some of them the natives were just flat-out slaves; but in a good part, the natives were serving and paying tribute to the 'gods' of the far suns."

"It's your damned transposers!" The engineer was exasperated. "I might even be able to swallow your starships coming back. But this transposer bit. Nah. What evidence—archaeological, historic, mythological, geological or any other damned logical—could you possible find for them?"

The archaeologist looked out at the stars—cold, bright, hard, in the cold dark sky. "Velikovsky outlined the evidence of the three catastrophes that show the transposer. He didn't know of the potential of the solar tap. The Van Allen belts hadn't even been discovered when he published, so he couldn't recognize and tie in the evidence of the Cheops pyramid or the palaces, or the obvious fact of electricity and a technological civilization existing as a superstructure over a primitive civilization. But he found the evidence of the catastrophes and their details and their effects. He published that evidence in three carefully documented volumes. He finally had to give credit to a comet as the cause, and he passed over all the factors that didn't pertain to a comet.

"The evidence that the natives—the hu-men—were used in the struggles between the various outsiders—the way we tried to use the Vietnamese to stop the spread of communism—is extensive. Take just the tribe of Moses and its 'ark' that must be carried everywhere with them and kept with the leader at all times. That tribe was directed by radio; the technological assistance it was given in conquering the cities and wiping out the people it was directed to conquer and wipe out—the assistance is obvious. And the fact that whoever was directing the tribes needed gold—probably to rebuild electronic equipment destroyed in the castastrophe—is obvious, too. He needed gold, and he needed to be fed under more sanitary conditions than prevailed. Read the rules he laid down!

"When you know about the solar tap, you know how the planetary engineering job to cause the flood was done. When you know about the flood, you know what happened at Sodom and Gomorrah, and begin to see why. When you know about Sodom and Gomorrah, you know someone here was getting ready to mine Mars. When you know that, you know that mining Mars was possible and that someone was doing it, and was mining the fifth planet, and that the fifth planet blew in 1450 B.C. When you know about that, you begin to deduce the transposer, and that it was in use between Egypt and Crete and Earth and Mars and the fifth planet, and when the transposer there blew, it blew secondarily on every one of the transposer sites. The hundred heads.

"When you deduce the transposer, you realize

that the basic theory simply takes the Einstein equations one step further. Then you estimate the amount of power needed to take the equations one step further, and your solar tap gives you sufficient power. And we have the technology of the solar tap right here, right now. So you realize that the transposer is not only possible but probable, and to us.

"And when you know that, and you look at the evidence of the flying saucers, you know that you have in your skies today both the landing craft from the big Vahs, and the small 'viewer' and 'fishing' transposers. And you figure that the interstellar transposers will be here again as soon as it can be arranged.

"And when you recognize those things, all the other factors begin to fall into place—the Aryans and the Minoans and the Aezier, the Vahsatans and the Vahsaba'alem and the Pharem—the Shiraphim and the Charubim. You know who they were and what they were, and you can just about pinpoint where they came from. You know why the palaces and temples were built the way they were, and what purposes the oddly placed doors and windows served.

"The palaces and the pagans; the Cretan and the Roman and the Pagan civilizations. The Vedic hymns and the stories of creation. The catastrophes and the brutalities; the learning and the growing and . . . the works."

"And we're the new race—the patsies—for all that?"

"Oh, we're not the only new race. As far as I know, we're the only ones that started from an evolutionary throwback. Call us the hu-man race, the clean-slate, re-evolution people, and you can distinguish the difference.

"But all the transposer people, and a good many of the Vahnire were 'new races' in effect—they were grown from colonists planted on far worlds; and though they started with a technology—as, in essence, so did we, or Lord David wouldn't have been able to create us—some of the planets must have been real brutal, and they went a long way back from what had been known on Atalama as 'civilization.' And remember, they didn't develop the transposer on those planets. They mostly had the solar tap to start with, but the transposer was developed right here, by the 'Old Ones' who took a few centuries of their new long lives to grow up slowly and do a job. The transposer people—the Charubim—got their advanced electronic gadgets right here. The spaceships that planted them came back here, found the transposer, and went back to put gates on the colony planets. And those colonists, now gone back to barbarianism or thereabouts, hit the culture growing here with all the brash, barbaric, brilliant, cocky ignorance of a child reaching the dress-up stage. Much as the Huns hit Rome, and with much the same results, except that the advanced electronic gadgets they found here made them much more lethal.

"All of them—the fifty late-come Titans, the Aryans, the Miners, the Vahsatans, the Vahsaba'al, the Wyzier . . . even the Olympians. New people, centuries — more than a thousand years — removed from the old civilization at Atalama.

They didn't evolve their own transposer technologies; they inherited them from the Old Ones who stayed after the flood and developed the transposer.

"Primitive culture, are we? The transposers that whichever of those colonists are back here now are using — those transposers were developed right here on Earth. Not by us, not by the hu-men; but by the ones I've been calling Pat Tos and Memph Luce and Zad Shara and Ted Promo and the other three who stayed with them and took time to grow up.

"The 'New Ones' inherited it. But we — we've developed, ourselves, the know-how you used to discover the solar tap. And we've home-grown the know-how that will give us regeneration in the next few decades. And we've home-grown the know-how that can give us the transposer before it's imposed on us — if we work fast enough.

"So — are we primitives?"

"Well," said the engineer, "are we primitives?"

"The guys in the 'saucers' think so." The archaeologist looked at the engineer almost pleadingly. "They're about to sell us the Brooklyn Bridge again, I think. They've come back to take stock of their two-legged 'animals'; to see about their 'marks', a carnie would call it.

"But we have got the home-grown, basic knowledges to develop on our own the technology that was the 'knowledge of the Lord.' We don't have to have it handed to us on a platter–not that they'd give it, as to subjects or children. Or suckers. We've got the know-how now to develop it on our own. Every one of those 'knowledges of the Lords.'

"The only question," he said softly, is: will we do it in time?"

The planet that showed in the viewscreen was a great golden ball, glowing with the fiery brilliance of sodium atoms in extreme electronic turmoil.

It's a ghastly color, though Zad, sitting quietly in the shadows at the side of the control room; feeling helpless that the work going on around her was not something in which she could join; sitting quietly with Memph, beside David who, in turn, was helpless beside Pat Tos as he used radio control to maneuver the tiny craft on the lashing seas below that held Noah and his family and a moderate variety of animals and birds and plants, and, above all, seeds.

The other tribes hadn't listened; had refused to take seriously the warnings of the Lord. Or, perhaps one or two of the tribes in the Andes had actually heeded the warning? Or the tribes in the tremendous lands far to the east of the guarded area? The tribes that called themselves Dravidians, and that they had finally decided were the descendants of the people that Bon Hindra had taken with him. These seemed to listen.

Zad and Memph and David had spent the year going from tribe to tribe, cautioning them, imploring them, warning them. The language barrier had been formidable; for every tribe outside the guarded area of the Aeton, the First One, had shown a new variation of the original old Atalaman. In each place they'd gone, they'd had to spend weeks getting into communication—overriding the fears that the tribes almost invariably showed—before they could even start trying to convince them that the warning was real, that the floods would comes; that mountain caves, even, might not be sufficient—though that would be better than nothing if they could not or would not build boats.

The trips had convinced Zad as nothing else could have that the catastrophic flood was a necessity if the new race was to survive at all. The twisted bodies, the freaks, the . . .

Zad turned her mind again to the golden ball on the viewscreen.

It was a special dispensation that had gotten Memph and her into the control room, rather than the big lounge where those not on duty watched the planetary engineering feat on a repeater screen. David had asked for them, and David's was an unquestioned right to be in the control room, beside Pat Tos, who was at the controls of the tiny ark as it rode out the violent storms below.

Telescopic observation had long since become impossible through the glowing, unnatural shroud that surrounded the planet. Even electronic signals were erratic, and Pat was guiding the ark more by the feel he had acquired over the past forty days than by actual electronic signals.

Has it really been forty days now, that the floods have risen and the rains have poured? Zad asked herself. Time had seemed to stand still as the great job went on; every member of the Vaheva was concentrated, with an intensity that seemed impossible, on the lives that hung in the balance on their ability to control the forces they had unleashed.

Beside her, Memph stirred and spoke quietly to

David. "You're going on with Enoch and his family to a new planet, aren't you, David?"

The other nodded, but didn't speak.

"Would you mind if I stayed with your people here? I wouldn't be a colony, just a guardian."

David looked at him in surprise. "It's lonely, " he said. "The Vaheva won't be back, you know, for twenty-two hundred years at the earliest."

"I know," said Memph. "But . . . there's work to be done. That I can't do aboard the Vaheva." Then, with a rush of words as though to get it out before he lost his courage, he said, "David, you've grown up. You've grown up in a way that—I don't think it's possible to grow up that way inside the— patterns of civilization. I think you need peace and quiet and elbow room, and time to get to know yourself and to know what life is like, to grow up that way. I want to grow up," he ended lamely.

David looked at him affectionately. "You don't think it's the added years that do it? You'll have regeneration aboard the Vaheva, you know."

Memph shook his head stubbornly. "I thought that at first, but I don't think so. It's not just the added years. It's the . . . perhaps the elbow room? I want to find out."

David nodded. "I think you're right," he said. "I should be very happy if you were here with them," and he gestured toward the dials that connected Pat to the big atomic motors they'd installed aboard the Ark.

Pat looked over at Memph. "You'll need an engineer," he said. "I'm staying too. I've been thinking about it all the past year."

Zad smiled happily. They might have been

reading her mind. She'd known for some time now what she wanted.

"You'll need a mentor," she said.

On the far side of the room, Ted Promo looked up from the meters and scopes and dials that for him spelled out the minute of the events below.

"Captain," he said formally, "I think we'd better release some of the retarder right away. It's getting pretty rough down there. We should slow it down."

Jeris Gavarel, standing at Promo's side, turned to Pat Tos. "How's the Ark?" he asked.

"It's holding well. I've got them as far from any land mass as I can. Those motors we installed are pretty good, but they're having a rough time in that storm, I'd wager."

"Where have you got them?" asked the captain.

"In the middle of the big sea west of the big inland lake . . . what was the big inland lake, and what was the big sea. It's all one sea with islands of mountains, now. They ought to ride it out without hitting anything there."

"Very well. Mr. Promo," said the captain formally, "release the first of the chlorine."

Promo's hand barely moved, but Zad could feel his tension; knew that the first of the storage domes of hydrogen and chlorine gases would have been triggered into activity by that slight motion.

In her mind's eye, she saw the natural rock cavity far below the surface of the ground into which chlorine and hydrogen had been forced under ever-increasing pressures, until at last the chlorine had begun to liquefy.

She had learned that chlorine and hydrogen are inert toward each other and may be mixed quite safely, so long as the mixture is kept dark. And that was the secret. Expose the mixture to light, and it reacts violently, explosively; and in large quantities, disastrously. So the fuse was the simple light bulb—or bulbs—that they had planned, designed to be keyed from this ship and to blow the various domes, one at a time, under perfect control. But one had blown while they were filling it, with a violent explosion that had shown her dramatically just what the explosion, occurring now on the planet below, was like; and leaving her with a tentative feeling about the remaining domes below—bombs waiting to be exploded.

"Number-one retarder released." Promo broke her train of thought. "The meter shows the explosion. We should see some of the reaction in about five minutes." He indicated the screen and sat back to wait.

Zad stared at the screen, at the glowing golden sphere which looked from this viewpoint to be seething with energies equivalent to those of the sun, though in actual fact, she knew that this was far from the truth.

"There it is," she muttered to herself, as a dark spot appeared, a slowly expanding circle that seemed rapidly to take on the shape and characteristics of a sunspot.

Promo sat forward abruptly and stared hard at the instruments that were repeating the electronic details of the story unfolding below. "I didn't expect *that* much effect," he said. Then, after a pause; "Captain, it's working *backward*."

Zad watched in fascination as a tall, fiercely glowing prominence rose from the center of the brown spot.

It's sticking out its tongue at us, she thought.

"It's putting out free protons!" Promo's voice was unhappy. Then: "And it's shaking things up down below, too. There's . . . damn! Captain. Number-two dome just went."

"Do you know what caused the second explosion, Mr. Promo?" The captain's voice hadn't changed, carried no inflection.

"No, sir. I don't know. It's damn touchy stuff, of course."

As he spoke, another of the green lights on his board flicked suddenly red. And then, in rapid succession, several more.

"Is there anything we can do to quiet the explosions, Mr. Promo?" The captain's voice was still calm.

"I don't know of anything, sir. I guess I just tell myself what a murdering idiot I am and wait to see what happens." His voice held a deep bitterness.

"Mr. Promo. There will be no self-recriminations." Then the captain allowed a small, wry smile onto his face, and his voice took a gentle overtone. "As far as I know, this is the first planetary engineering job. We could wish that it were a more perfect job," he said.

The hours passed and they watched while at increasingly frequent intervals the tiny telltale lights flicked from green to red, sometimes singly, more often in pairs, triplets, and chains. Only five out of nearly two hundred of the telltales still glowed green. And, shortly after each flick, another brownish circle began to spread, and then to put out its bright prominence of free hydrogen nuclei standing like a sword above its center of turbulence; until the ball, almost completely brown now, bristled with swords.

The room was quiet, interrupted only occasionally by the captain's query: "How is the Ark doing?" And Pat's intent answer, "The Ark is still fighting, sir. It's still afloat." And finally, Promo's bitter voice; "The brakes are going on now . . . fast. I—I don't think they've got a chance. It's almost all up there—and the brakes are going on."

Then Promo seized a pencil and did some rapid calculations. When he spoke, his voice was loud and fierce. "Pat," he said, "keep that Ark headed west." He paused and caught his breath, as though he'd been running hard. Then he went on, "There'll be a small tidal wave going west . . . and your tendency might be to turn the Ark to face into it. But don't do it. It should be followed by a giant wave—a really giant tidal wave—going east."

"I've got it headed west, Ted." Pat's voice was strained. "I've got it headed west at full power. How much time do you figure? But those are mighty puny motors."

"I . . . any time, now. Not for a few hours yet, I'd think."

Somebody brought coffee and sandwiches. Zad found herself eating, and realized she hadn't even noticed when her hand had picked up the the sandwich. The coffee was hot and tasted good. *Something to hang on to,* she thought.

"Here comes the first one, I think," said Pat in a

soft voice that carried throughout the control room in the silence.

Then . . . and Zad realized it was nearly an hour later, "Here's the second . . . " Had she been holding her breath all that time? *I couldn't have,* she thought.

"It's taking us . . . " Zad knew he meant the Ark. "It's taking us. I can't fight it. I—we're headed west, but . . ."

Then, "We're over land. We're . . . my god, what a wave that must be! The Ark is over the coast—it's being swept inland—we're heading—"

Only the instruments told the story: a wave that went three times around the planet; the tidal wave that, at one time, Promo estimated as at least 700 cubits tall, smashing and tearing at the mountain barriers in its path, speeding at at least 1,000 miles an hour. . . .

It was the first twenty-five hours that were the worst. By then the gigantic wave was losing weight, was losing speed. *Speed is a comparative figure,* Zad reminded herself.

Promo and Pat spelled each other at the controls of the Ark. No one thought of leaving the control room.

The picture on the viewscreen was changing now. The globe was still there, but it no longer had so much as a trace of the golden glow. And spotty, faint-blue tinges opened to show what must be seas. Flat blue plains.

The telescopic view was pinpointed and enlarged when the patches appeared, focusing on them to show madly churning seas and a few peaks of land, glistening with a new rocky whiteness. And finally, under now-scattering clouds, the last of the tidal wave as it spalshed its fury on the mountainous coastlines on the far side of the planet from the guarded area.

But the Ark was still afloat. Whether there would be life still aboard, they had no way of knowing yet. But it was still afloat, far inland, near a low range of hills, its motors still fighting.

Pat was at the controls of the Ark now, and he stood up suddenly. "The motors quit," he said. "They've had it." His voice was choked and he swallowed spasmodically, his fists clenching.

David stood beside him, put his arm gently around the young engineer's shoulders. "The wave's spent now," he said. "Is there any more coming, do you think, Ted?"

"No," said Promo wearily. "The worst is over now. I figure the planet's rotation is slowed at least twenty-five percent from its top speed. The rest should be gradual. David," he said. "We . . . "

"I know," David answered before the impossible sentence could trail to its end. "I know."

Zad watched until the Vaheva's landing craft disappeared into the deep blue of the skies above the island that would be their home. *Two years,* she thought. It took almost two years, but it's dry now.

Then her eyes wandered down to the calm inland sea that stretched beyond the horizon, wandered past the plastic bubble-domes that they had delightedly named the "New University at Créta," to the damp soil at her feet. To where . . .

Glossary

Atalama—the original civilization.

Aetala—the north; the arctic regions; also, the name of the "president" of Atalama.

Lama—the south; sea.

Ura—or Ur or Urath—the one continent of Atalama.

Baron Sivos—developer of the solar tap. It is possible that the title 'Baron' meant a doctorate in physics.

Siva—the solar tap; also known as

She or Shee-op—from the shee-gulp sound that it made.

The Vahs—the starships of old Atalama.

Vahnire—the people of the Vahs.

An, Ain, Amon, Aeton, Ur-Aenos—the First One. Lord David.

Aenia—the immortals. Also, Anunnaki; also Aengels.

Cha—transposer.

Cha-ran—users of the transposers; also guards of the transposers.

Ra—the sun; a sun; any sun.

Pha-ra—those who came from the far suns; the sons of the suns.

She-ra-phim—also Si-ra-phim. The people of the Sivas.

Nephilim—the crew of the Vaheva.

Cha-ra-bim—also Charubim. The transposer peoples.

Rg Vedic—the written Vahdic; the written word of the Vahnire.

Ankh—Crux Aensata—a spray hypodermic, or perhaps a needle hypodermic. Used in making people well. Used by the Vahsat'an in Lower Egypt.

Uraes—a symbol meaning representative of, or speaking for the 'aes" of old Ura—the immortals. Later came to mean the representative of, or speaking for whatever people of the suns was currently in power.

Gizeh, Giza—the fountain of light; the area from which comes the power.

Shi-nar, She-nar—without the She.

-sos, -stine, -tec—suffixes meaning descendants of and/or trained by the people named in the prefix; i.e., Aeztec, Pharostine, Wytchsos.

Wyzier—Warlords of the planet Wytch.

WS - #0097 - 120923 - C0 - 203/127/10 - PB - 9781479439041 - Gloss Lamination